# DELTA

**Shelby Delacroix**—lawyer, and youngest member of Delacroix and Associates. She has no idea she's about to be used as a pawn in a plot for revenge.

**Travis Hardin**—Texas rancher. He's come to Bayou Beltane looking for the truth about the mysterious death of his great-aunt.

**Roberta Hardin**—Travis's grandmother. She resurrects an age-old mystery.

**Justin Delacroix**—Shelby's father, and former senior partner at Delacroix and Associates. He's recently been appointed judge.

**Charles Delacroix**—Shelby's grandfather, a semi-retired lawyer, and former head of Delacroix and Associates.

**Yvette Avenall**—Shelby's childhood friend and new owner of 'The Book Nook'.

# SILHOUETTE BOOKS

*proudly presents*

**12 stories featuring the privileged Delacroix family**

# DELTA JUSTICE

**A wealthy family dynasty is shattered by a
mysterious crime of passion...
Can the power of love save them?**

| | |
|---|---|
| **Contract: Paternity** | Jasmine Cresswell |
| **Letters, Lies & Alibis** | Sandy Steen |
| **Finding Kendall** | Anne Logan |
| **In the Bride's Defence** | Kelsey Roberts |
| **Every Kid Needs a Hero** | Candace Schuler |
| **Son of the Sheriff** | Sandy Steen |
| **Overruled by Love** | MJ Rodgers |
| **Someone to Watch Over Her** | Kelsey Roberts |
| **For the Love of Beau** | Margaret St George |
| **French Twist** | Margot Dalton |
| **Legacy of Secrets** | Judith Arnold |
| **Desires and Deception** | Penny Richards |

# Letters, Lies & Alibis

# SANDY STEEN

SILHOUETTE®

*Silhouette and Colophon are registered trademarks of
Harlequin Books S.A., used under licence.*

*First published in Great Britain 2003.
Silhouette Books, Eton House, 18-24 Paradise Road,
Richmond, Surrey TW9 1SR*

© Harlequin Books S.A. 1997

*Special thanks and acknowledgement are given to Sandra Steen
for her contribution to the Delta Justice series.*

ISBN 0 373 82562 5

*142-1003*

*Printed and bound in Spain
by Litografía Rosés S.A., Barcelona*

## SANDY STEEN

Hooked on romance since she was twelve, Sandy credits dedicated teachers who stressed the benefits of a solid reading foundation for a major part of her success. Since her first book was published, she has become a bestselling author and an award winner. A native Texan, Sandy leads a busy life as an author, wife, mother and grandmother. But most of all, she is a lover of romance in print, on the screen, and, of course, in real life.

Dear Reader,

Whenever people speak of the South, certain familiar images come to mind, particularly of Louisiana. Images of sparkling white plantation homes, beautiful Southern belles in hoop-skirted dresses and sweet-scented magnolias. It may be part of our pop culture, but it's also part of our history. It reminds us of a time when a gentleman's honour was his most prized possession, his family name his most revered and protected treasure. DELTA JUSTICE is about a family that has deep roots in that time. A family that has weathered wars, heartbreak and bitterness, but not without some scars and secrets that have shaped the lives of at least three generations.

I hope you find the Delacroix as fascinating to read about as I did to write about. They're a collection of proud, passionate...and ruthless characters. Just the mixed bag of characterisation most writers long for.

Sincerely,

*Sandy Steen*

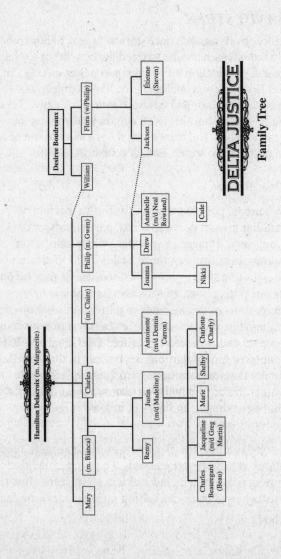

DELTA JUSTICE
Family Tree

# PROLOGUE

TRAVIS HATED HOSPITAL rooms. Hated their cramped spaces, their cold, sterile interiors, the way they smelled. Most of all he hated the fact that they were, more often than not, waiting rooms for death and dying. Like now.

Was it only yesterday, he wondered, sitting forward in the singularly uncomfortable chair, that his grandmother had suffered a totally unexpected heart attack? It seemed like a week ago. Surely days had passed since she had walked into the kitchen of the Hardin ranch and announced that she didn't feel well enough to go to church. Travis dug the heels of his hands into his eyes and rubbed. He should have realized anything serious enough to keep her away from Sunday services was serious enough to warrant immediate attention. If only he hadn't let her talk him out of calling the doctor. If he had just insisted...

But he hadn't. Two hours later she'd been filling a glass with water at the kitchen sink and had collapsed. Paramedics had rushed her to the hospital, where doctors performed emergency open heart surgery to correct an almost ninety percent blockage.

*Stable.* That's the word the cardiologist had used when he spoke to Travis and his dad outside the ICU. She was stable, but not completely out of the woods. Twelve hours later she had been weaned from the ventilator but was still sedated, and still in the ICU being closely watched for a possible pulmonary embolism, or in layman's terms, a blood clot. A tiny glob of blood that could kill her.

Travis rose and walked to the foot of her bed. "It isn't fair, Gran," he whispered. "You don't deserve this."

He wanted to rage, strike out at something. Anything. One of the two people that mattered most to him was lying helplessly hooked up to heart and pulse monitors, catheters and God knew what else, and there wasn't one damned thing he could do about it. Despite his grandmother's indomitable spirit and strong will, the odds were not in her favor. Travis couldn't even begin to imagine what his life would be like without her.

He'd been six when his mother had been killed by a drunk driver, and his father's leg had been injured in the same accident. His memories of his mother were mostly from old photographs and stories his father had related. Gran was the only mother he had ever really known. She had cooked, cleaned, worked side by side with his father on the ranch and still found the time to take a shy boy and give him the confidence he needed to become a man. She had been there for him, steadfast, strong and loving in all the moments of his life, good and bad. From his performance as Rudolph the Red-Nosed Reindeer in his first-grade Christmas pageant, through high school graduation, to the day he had taken over the operation of the ranch with his father's blessing. As faded as his memories were of his mother, memories shared with Gran were clear and indelible. The day he learned to ride a horse, then a bicycle, and she was ready both times with iodine and bandages. The pride on her face at his Eagle Scout presentation. The "few dollars" she had tucked away so he could take his date to the senior prom someplace nice for dinner. Gran's values and morals were his. Along with his dad, she was the foundation of his life.

And Travis loved her more than anyone on the face of the earth.

Now, watching her sleep, he was stunned at how old she looked. When had her hair become almost white? When had this woman who seemed so ageless and indestructible become so frail? So mortal? He realized how much he had taken her presence in his life for granted. His man's mind knew she was only human, but his boy's heart had hoped she would live forever. There was nothing he wouldn't do for her. Even now, if his own heart would extend her life, he would gladly give it.

"Trav?" He glanced up as his dad came into the room, two cups of coffee in a cardboard tray in one hand, his cane in the other.

Travis took a cup. "Thanks, Dad." He grimaced after his first swallow of the machine-brewed coffee. "This stuff is thick enough to stand on its own."

"And talk back." T.C. took a sip, then made his way to the side of his mother's bed. "How's she doin'?"

"About the same. Once in a while she stirs and acts like she might be coming around, but then she drifts off again. Sometimes she mumbles, but nothing I can understand."

"You think she's in a lot of pain?"

"I don't know, Dad. Hope not."

T.C. nodded. Leaning on his cane for support, he

patted his mother's hand. "Mama?" he said softly. "Mama, it's T.C. Travis is here, too. The nurses think maybe you can hear, so we're gonna keep talking till you wake up, you hear?" He gave her hand one last pat, then turned to claim the only other chair in the room.

Roberta Hardin moaned. Instantly, both men were at her side. She moaned again, licked her dry lips, but didn't open her eyes.

"You talk to her, Trav. She's always had a soft spot for your sweet talk." T.C. managed a weak smile. "But don't you let on I told you."

As Travis pulled the chair up next to her bed, he thought of the first day she had come to live at the ranch. He had sweet-talked her into baking cookies, but to this day she insisted that had been her intention all along. It was years before he knew how difficult it had been for her to return to the ranch she and her husband had built in Comfort, near San Antonio, where Tom Hardin had died only five years earlier after being thrown from a horse. At that point, Gran had signed everything over to Travis's dad and mother, and moved to San Antonio, because the memories were too painful. But when his mother died and his dad lay injured, she had returned, and stayed. She had simply dealt with what life handed her and did the best she could for her son and grandson. He and Gran had bonded the day she returned in a way they never had before. Maybe it was because she knew about loss firsthand. Or maybe it was because instinctively he knew she had given up a lot to care for a lonely little boy.

Gently, he lifted her hand. "Hey, darlin'. How's

my best girl? Dad and I are just waiting for you to open those gorgeous blue eyes and smile at…"

Suddenly her eyelids fluttered. "Dad," Travis called. "I think she's waking up."

T.C. was beside him almost before Travis finished speaking.

"Sor…ry," Roberta said in a papery whisper.

"What is it, Mama? Do you need something?"

She licked her dry lips in an effort to speak as she struggled into consciousness. T.C. grabbed a mug of water with a bendable straw and offered her a drink, but she turned away.

"Sor-ry," she whispered. "Cam…Camille."

The sound of the name made Travis's blood run cold. His grandmother was calling the name of her sister, dead for almost sixty years. The hair stood up on the back of his neck.

"No, Mama, it's—"

"Dad, she's not awake."

"But—"

"It's like before. I don't think she knows what she's saying."

"S-scared," she murmured. "Too late…now. Poor little…poor little Camille."

"It's all right, Gran," Travis said, trying to soothe her. She moaned, then drifted off again.

That pattern continued through the night, with Travis and T.C. taking turns at her bedside. Then shortly before dawn, while T.C. made another coffee run, she stirred again.

"I'm here, Gran," Travis said, holding her hand.

For the first time she opened her eyes. As she turned her head toward him, her thin, wrinkled hands reached up and clutched at his shirt. Her fingers tangled in the fabric as she made a weak attempt to pull him closer.

"Murdered her. My sweet Camille. Never should have...kept quiet." She shook her head. "Mis-mistake."

"Gran—" Travis smacked the call button for the nurse's station "—you need to stay calm. Let me—"

"There's proof," she insisted, her gaze fixed on Travis. "You have to do it for me. Find the truth. Promise me, Travis. Promise."

"I promise, only please, Gran, you've got to rest—"

"Camille?" Her gaze slid past her grandson. "You forgive me, don't you, Camille?"

Then she smiled, as if she had received the answer she'd been hoping for. A second later she slumped back against the pillow and the heart monitor alarm sounded. Then the alarm on every piece of medical equipment seemed to go off at once. The door to the room burst open and suddenly doctors were barking orders, nurses were hustling around. T.C. limped in behind them. After that, the only thing Travis remembered was his father in the midst of all the commotion, silent tears running down his cheeks.

# CHAPTER ONE

"DAD, THERE'S NO RUSH to do this. It's only been three weeks."

T. C. Hardin glanced around him at the cardboard boxes, some already full of clothing that had belonged to his mother. "No. I can't stand the thought of walking past this room every day. But it's harder than I expected."

"There's no rule that says you have to be the one to clear out Gran's things."

"I'm her son. I should—"

"Dad, let me do this for you."

Briefly, the elder Hardin closed his eyes, then put a hand on his son's shoulder. "Thanks." He turned and left.

Dreading the job that lay before him, yet knowing the sooner it was done the better his father would feel, Travis stepped into his grandmother's room.

The spacious bedroom, complete with a fireplace, had once been the main room of the original cottage, built more than fifty years ago. The room and everything in it bore the indelible stamp of his grandmother's personality: soft trappings, pleasing to the eye, but beneath it all, substance. Organdy curtains draping the bay window were slightly yellowed with age but had been freshly washed and starched shortly before her death. On the four-poster bed was her patchwork quilt, a wedding gift, in varying shades of lilac, faded now to whiteness along most of the hand-stitched seams but laundered the same day as the curtains. Here and there were touches of lace, crocheted doilies, heirlooms from her mother.

Frillies, Gran had called them. A woman had to have her frillies, she insisted, or she just didn't feel like a woman. Travis couldn't remember a time when she hadn't carried a lace-trimmed handkerchief in the pocket of even her most well-worn cotton dress, or when she hadn't smelled of her favorite lilac fragrance. Her hands might have been callused from a lifetime of hard work, but her touch was infinitely gentle. She was soft-spoken, well mannered and compassionate. A lady from the ground up.

But if one part of the room spoke to the true character of Roberta Hardin, it was the furniture. All of it—bed, night table, chifforobe, vanity and cheval mirror—was solid oak. Sturdy, well crafted and passed down through at least three generations, it had endured gracefully. As had she, a strong woman with a tender heart.

How often had he sat in this room as a child and listened to stories of her youth spent along the north shore of Lake Pontchartrain in southern Louisiana? Hundreds, probably. Maybe even thousands. The stories always centered around her sister, Camille, their years together and Camille's untimely death. Gran had never gotten over the loss, and had often claimed the wrong man had been convicted for Camille's murder.

Travis turned away, the pain of remembering almost too sharp to bear. He fought the urge to walk out and lock the door forever. But he wouldn't, of course. He forced himself to walk across the room, pick up one of the boxes and set it on the bed. Then he opened the closet and went to work.

Two hours later he had sorted through most of his grandmother's clothing and had started on her vanity. He sat down on the stool, feeling ridiculous and awkward seated in front of the array of powders, lipsticks and creams. This was the hardest part. Everything here was so personal. The perfume atomizer she had used forever. Her jewelry box, still open from the last time she had used it, and containing pieces of costume jewelry she had favored. And her handkerchiefs, all neatly pressed in a drawer to themselves. The longer he sat there, the harder it was to keep the memories at bay, particularly of her last moments. Now he was packing away mementos of a lifetime, sick at heart that his grandmother had left this world so obviously troubled. He reached for a brooch she had worn to church the last Sunday before she died, then stopped, suddenly unable to go through these things item by item. He grabbed one of the smaller packing boxes and emptied the contents of the drawers into it. Closing the jewelry box, he set it inside as well, then added the atomizer and other things, literally raking them into the box with his hand. When everything was packed away, he took several deep, steadying breaths.

It was so strange, he thought, to see the vanity bare. He ran his fingertips over the surface, enjoying the feel of the wood grain. As he did, he looked around at the other pieces. They didn't make furniture like this anymore, and despite the obvious wear, the bedroom set, once refinished, would be not only handsome but serviceable for many more years.

The idea of restoring the furniture brought Travis a measure of comfort. He would do the work himself, of course, and afterward they could set it up in the spare bedroom rather than put it in storage, where it would just become dry and cracked.

He stood up and walked to first one piece, then another, inspecting each for damage. As he'd expected, all of it was structurally sound and would require only a little sanding and a couple of coats of varnish. Everything but the cheval mirror. When he checked the mirror's ornate pivot, he discovered that the frame was loose. So much the better. It would have to come apart to be refinished, and in the meantime he would take it into San Antonio to have it resilvered. Almost lovingly, he withdrew the brackets holding the pivot, then lifted the mirror to put it on the bed.

As he did, several sheets of pale pink paper slipped from between the mirror and the backing and fluttered to the floor like dry leaves in an autumn breeze. Odd, he thought, laying the huge oval mirror facedown on the bed. He picked up the sheets of paper and discovered they were...

Letters?

Three in all, addressed to Bobbie, a long-ago nickname of his grandmother's, all written in a dainty, feminine script, and all signed "Your loving sister, Camille."

Travis couldn't believe it. Such a strange coincidence to find them now. More like bizarre, considering his grandmother's last words. As it had that day, the hair on the back of his neck stood up, and he couldn't shake the feeling that finding the letters was no coincidence at all.

"Too much grief and too little sleep, cowboy," he whispered. "You're letting your imagination run wild."

They were just old letters his grandmother had probably thought she'd lost years ago. More than likely they contained nothing but chatty news. A touch uncomfortable with handling letters not addressed to him, he started to put them in the box with the other personal items, glancing at the dates as he did so. The first one had been written May 21, 1938, the second, May 28, and the last, June 8.

A date he knew by heart because it was the day Camille Gravier had died.

Now, compelled to learn the contents of the letters, Travis read each one twice. By the time he'd finished, he was torn between wanting to cry and wanting to smash something.

T.C. WAS IN THE DEN, staring into a cold fireplace, his hands in his pockets, when Travis walked in with the letters. "What's that?" T.C. asked.

"Letters to Gran, from her sister, Camille."

"Are you serious? Where in the world did you get 'em?"

"I decided to have Gran's furniture restored, and when I took the mirror apart these fell out." He handed his dad the first letter. "She must have hidden them there."

"Why would she do a fool thing like that?"

"Just read it, Dad."

When T.C. finished reading, Travis handed him the second letter. "My God," T.C. said when he got to the end.

"You didn't know Camille was pregnant when she was killed? Gran never mentioned it?"

A little stunned, T.C. shook his head and sat down on the sofa. "I had no idea. She never said a word."

"There's more." Travis began to read the last letter.

Dear Bobbie,

I know I sounded scared the last time I wrote you, but I think things are going to be all right now.

I'm meeting Charles tonight out by the lake, and he promised he would fix everything. I know the Delacroix are the richest people in the parish, and I know folks will say I did it to trap him, but I swear, Bobbie, it's not true. Guess tongues are bound to wag, and some folks will believe the worst, no matter what.

Thank goodness Charles isn't like that. Except for losing his temper once in a while, he's always treated me real good. Who knows? Maybe by the time you get this letter, I'll be engaged, and all this worry will be for nothing. Please come home as soon as you can, Bobbie.

                                        Your loving sister,
                                        Camille

Travis tossed the letter on top of the others on the coffee table in front of his father. "Dad, all these years when Gran said they convicted the wrong man of her sister's murder, she had evidence that would implicate Charles Delacroix. Right here, and in Camille's own handwriting. Why didn't she use it?"

"I—I don't know." Wearily, T.C. scrubbed his face with his hands. "Maybe..."

"What?"

"Maybe she didn't think anyone would believe her."

"But that doesn't make any sense. Any police department would see these as an indication of motive. She was carrying the man's baby, for Pete's sake."

T.C. thought for a moment. "The only reason I can come up with is that she wanted to protect Camille. Protect her reputation."

"Because of the baby, you mean?"

"Son, you're thinking like all this happened last week, or even last year, but it happened almost sixty years ago. You gotta remember things were different then, not like they are today. Back then, a woman having a baby outta wedlock was a real scandal. Mama loved her sister somethin' fierce. She would've done anything to protect her, and the rest of her family, too. I figure she probably hid these letters so her folks wouldn't find them."

"But after Camille died she could have gone to the law—"

"And dragged her dead sister's reputation through the mud? It took your grandmother years to be able to deal with Camille's death. By that time, the thought of raking up all the ugliness and gossip must have been more than she could handle. You know how she felt about airin' dirty linen in public. No. I think the last thing she wanted was to make a bad situation worse."

That much was true enough. Roberta Gravier Hardin had been an intensely private person and fiercely protective of all her family.

"A lot of things make sense now."

"You mean the things Gran said just before she…died."

"Yeah. Did she ever talk about that time? Specifically, I mean."

"When I was little, she used to tell me how much she loved Bayou Beltane, the place where she was born. But her daddy lost his job and they had to move to Texas after Camille was killed. Sometimes Mama would cry because she said she couldn't ever go back there. After a while she stopped talkin' about it. By the time you came along, I think she decided to remember only the good things about her sister. She loved to tell you those stories of when they were girls. The rest she just put out of her mind."

"I don't think it was ever far from her mind, Dad. It must have been more important than either of us knew, or she wouldn't have been almost…obsessed with it at the end."

T.C. picked up the letters and stacked them neatly. "It's the past. Dead and buried." He stood up and handed the letters to Travis. "Nothin' we can do about it," he said, and left the room.

But Travis was haunted by the letters and his grandmother's last words. And by his promise.

At the time he hadn't even known what he was promising, but what mattered was that Gran had died believing he would find the truth. And he would if he had to move heaven and earth to do it, starting with some research.

Thanks to fax machines, by that night Travis had in his possession not only a history and who's who of the Delacroix family, but also a copy of a lengthy newspaper article from the *Slidell Sentinel* and a smaller one from the *New Orleans Times-Picayune* covering the murder and trial. After dinner he went to his father.

"I'm going to Bayou Beltane."

"To do what?"

"Find the truth." He showed him the copy of the article. "They convicted a man named Rafael Perdido. Supposedly, he was crazy in love with Camille, but she wouldn't give him a tumble. He followed her out to the lake that night, and when he saw her with Charles Delacroix, he snapped. If he couldn't have her, no one would."

"And you don't think that's the truth?"

"The truth can be twisted, Dad. Don't you think it's a bit of a coincidence that Charles Delacroix and his sister, Mary, were witnesses for the prosecution, yet their father, Hamilton Delacroix, defended Perdido? Who, by the way, was a penniless drifter. And that's not all. It seems Hamilton Delacroix was just about the best lawyer in the state back then. Real high-powered, and got top dollar."

"Thought you said Perdido was penniless."

"Delacroix took the case pro bono."

T.C. sat up straighter. "How generous."

"Wasn't it?"

"For all the good it did the kid he was defendin'."

"Yeah. And here's the clincher. It's the only murder case Hamilton Delacroix ever lost."

"Are you sayin' he let Perdido hang to protect his son?"

"Perdido never made it to the gallows. He was killed in Angola Prison. And yeah, I think there's too many coincidences in all of this. Let's face it, money and power beat out dirt poor every time. And don't forget, Camille mentioned that Charles had a temper."

"So, you're thinkin' ole Charles's solution to the problem was to get rid of Camille, and Perdido happened to be in the wrong place at the wrong time."

"Then rich daddy steps in to help send the wrong man up the river. A shiftless kid with no money and no family against the parish gentry."

"Poor bastard didn't stand a chance."

"Exactly."

"But, Travis, what can you do about all of this now?"

"Maybe nothing, but think of all the years Gran suffered over this. No, Dad, this has to be set right. I'm going to keep my promise. Come hell or high water, I'm going to find the man who really murdered Great-aunt Camille."

"Well, I'm not gonna try to talk you out of it," T.C. said. "If what you suspect is true, the Delacroix have caused a lot of misery. Can't say the taste of revenge wouldn't be sweet knowin' they got what was comin' to them."

"Revenge?"

"Isn't that what we're talkin' about? To make 'em pay for what they did. To get justice."

"Yeah," Travis said, remembering how often Gran had quoted the verse *Revenge is mine, saith the Lord.* "I guess it is." He wondered if she had finally given up waiting for God to finish the task.

"Then, you need a plan, son. You got to think about what you'll do with the truth."

"I'll take whatever information I find to the district attorney. I'm not sure about Louisiana, but I don't think there's a statute of limitations on murder."

"You want to send Charles Delacroix to jail?"

"If he's a murderer, yes."

"Man must be in his late seventies or early eighties by now. I doubt he'd spend much time in jail."

That hadn't occurred to Travis. "So, you're saying I should forget about this?"

"No. I'm sayin' you need to hit 'em where it'll do the most damage—in their pride. Make them see what it's like to have everybody talkin' about 'em, wonderin', even judgin' 'em the way they did poor Camille. That'd knock 'em down a peg or two."

Travis thought about that for a moment, and an idea began to take shape. The Delacroix had their reputation to protect.

"You know, Dad, I think you just gave me my plan."

"How's that?"

"From the background information in the faxes, we know the Delacroix are upstanding citizens, right? Always getting their names in the society column, the business section."

"So?"

Travis looked at his father. "I wonder how they'd like to see the family name splashed across a tabloid or two?"

"Son, you can't just go to one of those tabloids with nothing more than Mama's letters and start making accusations. I don't want you leavin' yourself open to a slander suit. No matter what you promised Mama, she wouldn't want you to lose everything you've worked for on her account."

"Don't worry, Dad. The Delacroix have claimed their last victim in this family. The first thing I'm gonna do is hire a detective to get some in-depth background on Charles.''

"Why don't you just let the detective handle the whole thing?''

"Because I promised Gran. And because I want to see these people. See how they live, how they do business. Once I've got the proof, then I'll let the experts take over.''

"Experts?''

"Just think of what one of those tabloid reporters could do with proof that one of Louisiana's most influential citizens was guilty of murder. Even the sleazy operators protect their sources. The detective I hire can turn over the information. All we have to do is step back and watch the fireworks.''

"There you go,'' T.C. said. "Sounds like a plan.''

# CHAPTER TWO

AS MUCH AS SHELBY DELACROIX hated to admit it, she was jealous. Well, maybe *envious* was a better word. Not that she didn't wish her aunt Toni and Brody Wagner all the happiness in the world. She adored Toni, and Brody was a good friend and colleague. But seeing them now, gazing at each other as if the rest of the world didn't exist, Shelby wondered if she would ever have that kind of intimacy in her own life. And if envy wasn't enough, she might as well add voyeurism to her list of sins, because as painful as it was to watch them, she couldn't stop.

On her way from the conference room with a message for Brody, she had caught sight of them standing together in the doorway to his office. Shelby had stopped and stared. Their bodies were pressed close, and Toni had the same look in her eyes that she did when she was on stage, pouring her soul into a blues song. The look was sultry, intimate, and it made Shelby pointedly aware of the inadequacies in her own personal life.

Of course, to hear her family talk, she was too picky when it came to men. But then, they didn't know what she had gone through three years ago.

No one in her family did.

The Delacroix were great at helping other people out of their troubles, both legal and financial, but they couldn't seem to help one another. So Shelby had found her own strength. It hadn't been easy—her self-esteem had definitely been bruised—but she'd come out stronger. Now she knew what she wanted in a man, and what she didn't want. She longed for the intimacy and depth of commitment she saw when she looked at Toni and Brody, and when the right man came along, she'd have it. One thing was for certain—the man of her dreams had to be trustworthy.

Feeling as if she was trespassing, she cleared her throat.

Toni glanced around Brody's shoulder and smiled. "Hello, Shel."

"Hi, Toni. Hey, Brody."

"Hello, Shelby. How's the bright, new Delacroix legal eagle this morning?"

"Working my tail feathers off."

Brody smiled. "It'll pay off. You're going to be a star one these days."

Shelby looked at Toni. "You're getting a really sweet man. You know that, don't you?"

Toni smiled. "You better believe it."

"Listen, Brody, I hate to interrupt such a cozy tête-à-tête, but that pit bull you hired—"

Brody grinned. "You mean Cal Rockford?"

"Rockhead, if you ask me. I've never met anyone so obstinate or pushy. And can't you talk to him about those ties he wears? Personal style is one thing. Bad taste is something else."

Toni laughed. "No, really, Shel, how do you feel about this guy?"

"Don't worry," Brody reassured her. "As soon as he apprentices here for six months, I'm bringing him to New Orleans to work with me."

"Thank God! Maybe then he'll stop asking me out."

Brody enjoyed teasing Shelby and couldn't resist the opportunity. "Of course, you could go out with him. That would probably put a stop to his asking for sure."

Her eyes widened, and she opened her mouth to give a suitable reprimand when the intercom buzzed in his office.

"Saved by the bell," he said, and turned toward his office door. Before he could escape, Toni grabbed a handful of his tie and tugged. She gave him a quick kiss. "See you later," he murmured, and kissed her back, then stepped into his office.

"I take back what I said about you being sweet," Shelby called after him.

Toni laughed, then said to Shelby, "Are you headed back to your office?"

"Actually, I'm done for the day."

"Then, come on," she said, linking arms with her vivacious niece. "Walk me to my car."

The two of them chatted amiably about Toni's wedding plans all the way to the door. "So tell me," Toni said once they were outside, "is this Rockhead guy really obnoxious? Or is he getting to you because maybe you're a little attracted to him?"

"Pul-ease." Shelby rolled her eyes. "Nothing could be further from the truth. I've told him point blank to forget it."

"Point blank?"

"Absolutely. I don't play games. It's wrong to mislead a man into thinking he's got a chance when he doesn't. It's lying, plain and simple."

"Trust me, Shelby. There's nothing plain or simple

about the male-female relationship. And I was just wondering about Rockford, because you haven't really had a steady boyfriend since you started working at the firm.''

"You sound about as subtle as Aunt Mary, the family matchmaker. It's not that I lack for suitors, as she calls them. In fact, I date fairly often. Usually not the same man twice.''

"And why is that?''

Shelby leaned close to Toni and lowered her voice as if she were about to reveal the ultimate secret. "Confidentially, the men in this town are boring.''

"No kidding!'' Toni said, her own voice lowered. "Why do you think I left?''

They both laughed. "Actually,'' Shelby said, "it has more to do with time than lack of interest. I've been working night and day on a case that's just winding down.''

"Hope I wasn't out of line asking. I wasn't trying to be nosy—''

Shelby smiled. "Sure you were, but it's okay.''

They stopped walking, and Toni grasped her niece's hand. "Lord, I never thought I'd hear myself say this, but I just want you to be as happy as I am. And I don't want you to have to wait as long as I did to find happiness.''

"I understand, and I really do appreciate it. I'm just not the kind to go beating the bushes looking for Mr. Right.''

"Give Aunt Mary the job. She's pretty good at it.''

"Believe me,'' Shelby said, "she's on the case.''

"And?'' Toni held up her hand. "Forget I asked. If anyone knows how embarrassing those dates can be, I do.''

"She's so sweet, and her heart is in the right place, but…"

"Well, three months ago I would have said run, don't walk, the next time she finds you a date, but look what happened when I met Brody."

"You got lucky."

Toni sighed. "Boy, did I ever," she agreed, then added as they reached her car, "All right. I can tell when to drop a subject."

"Thanks. So, getting back to the wedding, how many guests *are* you planning on?"

"Don't get me started on that! This thing is getting out of hand. I'm trying to talk Brody into eloping. I keep telling him the sooner we get married the sooner I can get pregnant."

"Just think of it." Shelby sighed. "A tiny Delacroix-Wagner. We haven't had a baby in the family since Uncle Philip's daughter Annabelle gave birth to Cade."

"I think about it a lot. Maybe too much."

"Why do you say that?"

"I don't know, it's just that sometimes I scare myself thinking about the awesome responsibility of caring for a child." Toni smiled wistfully. "Then I think about how sweet my goddaughter Josie is, how wonderful it is just to hear her laugh, see her smile."

Despite the fact that members on both sides of the family often considered Toni to be frivolous and self-indulgent, Shelby knew different. She wished they could see Toni now, her eyes filled with compassion, her voice with longing.

Shelby reached out and squeezed Toni's hand. "You'll make a great mother."

"Oh, I don't know about great, but I want to be."

"No, trust me. You've got what it takes."

"And that is?"

"A lot of love to give. And most of all, commitment. You'll be there for your children no matter what."

Toni looked into her niece's eyes. "Yes, I will. Brody and I love each other, and we're willing to give three hundred percent to each other and our children."

"Hang on to that, Toni. So often couples forget the commitment they started out with."

"Are you thinking of your parents' divorce?"

"Unfortunately, I'm thinking of a lot of parents. Occupational hazard."

The subject of her parents was not one Shelby relished discussing. She had confronted that area of her life with the aid of therapy, but it still contained some shadowy corners. None of which she could tell Toni. No one in the family was aware that Shelby had ever consulted a therapist, must less seen one regularly during her senior year of law school. It wasn't that the Delacroix were unenlightened, they simply thought problems should be dealt with within the family. Her parents' divorce, when she was seventeen, was a prime example.

"All I know is that they probably started out feeling the same way you and Brody do, and look what happened to them."

"But…" Toni stopped herself. "Are you believing this? Me, trying to give advice to anyone on how to live her life? I've *got* to get back to New Orleans and stay there for a while. This small-town stuff is contagious."

Shelby laughed. "I think you're well vaccinated, Toni."

"Thank goodness Brody is in charge of the firm's satellite office not far from Chanson Triste. From now on the only reason we'll have to come to Bayou Beltane is to visit Aunt Mary. And I like it that way."

"Just think of all the gossip you'll miss."

"Yeah. Just think."

"Speaking of gossip, did you know Jax was home?"

"No." Toni smiled with delight. "That scamp. I can't believe she didn't let me know. She used to write occasionally when she was in Europe, but I haven't heard from her lately."

"I'm going out to the stables shortly. Want to join me and say hello?"

"Can't. This afternoon I'm interviewing a new musician for the Sunday brunch performance. Besides, I haven't been on horseback in ages, so it probably wouldn't be a good idea while I'm trying to conceive. Tell your sister that I said hello, and to call me."

"I will," Shelby promised. "But you know Jax. If you don't have hooves and a mane, she has very little time for you."

Smiling, Toni climbed into her car and stuck her head out the window as she backed out of her parking space. "Tell her I want to give all of my soon-to-be children riding lessons. That'll get her attention." And she drove away.

The encounter with Toni left Shelby feeling strangely restless and out of sorts. And she suddenly remembered that neither she nor Toni had mentioned the promise they made to Aunt Mary. It was probably better that way. What she needed was an invigorating

ride to clear her head and get rid of some tension.
Her sister had always insisted there was nothing that
couldn't be improved by a good gallop with a fine
horse. Shelby decided it was exactly what she needed.
She climbed into her own car and headed home.

*Home,* she thought as she maneuvered her sporty
Miata along the road leading to Riverwood. Since getting her degree and passing the bar, she'd had a lot
of trouble feeling like any place was home in the
sense that she was truly comfortable. Perhaps *secure*
was a better word.

There were few truths or elements of security
Shelby could still cling to with certainty, but being a
lawyer was one of them. She liked the law because it
helped make sense of a sometimes senseless world,
and because knowing she had a part, albeit small, in
helping justice prevail was what kept her grounded.
For Shelby, the law was more than a profession. It
was her life. At least for the present. But Toni's questions about having a special man in her life had struck
a definite chord. Lately, she had found herself deliberately avoiding thinking too far into the future, for
fear it would cast a glaring light on her lonely present.

Not that her life was devoid of loving people, because it wasn't. Her father, Justin, was a caring man.
And although he hadn't always been the most doting
parent when she and her siblings were younger, now
that they were adults he made time for each of them
despite his demanding duties as a newly appointed
federal judge. Shelby knew that her brother, Beau,
and her sisters, Charly, Jax and Marie, loved her. But
displays of affection were not exactly a family trait.
Pride, yes, loyalty, always, but rarely did they openly
express love toward one another. Shelby's grandfather

had set the pattern, and so far, no one had seen fit to alter it. The only exception was her great-aunt Mary, and even she favored moderation.

Well, Shelby reminded herself, she was home in Bayou Beltane, surrounded by her family, doing the work she loved. Nothing else mattered. Shoving her earlier thoughts about love and romance aside, she whipped the little convertible onto the lane leading to Riverwood, the family homestead, and focused on the enjoyment her ride would bring. After parking the car, she hurried inside, and fifteen minutes later, wearing jeans and a T-shirt she strolled into the stables.

Robert Bearclaw, a Cherokee Indian and head trainer of Delacroix Farms, looked up from repairing some tack. For more than forty years he had been involved with breeding and training Delacroix Thoroughbreds, starting as a stable boy and rising to manager. His skill with horses was legendary in Louisiana, and he had been a major contributor to the unqualified success of the operation. But he was more than an employee. He had taught all of the Delacroix children on both sides of the family to ride, and more important, he had taught them to respect the animals they rode. Bear was a constant, solid presence in Shelby's life, and in many ways had been more of a grandfather to her than her own. It was Bear who'd given her her first lecture about kissing, after catching her and the star receiver for the junior high school football team in an adolescent clinch.

"Hello, Bear."

"I was beginning to think you had given up horses and old Indians for good," he said, his broad, weathered hands never ceasing their work.

"It's been a while, I know, but I've been busy."

"Too busy, if you ask me. You can't carry the burden of breathing Delacroix blood back into that law firm all by yourself."

Shelby stiffened. Bear never minced words, and he had an uncanny way of knowing what was on her mind, and why. He had been reading her like a book all of her life, but sometimes, like now, it was irritating. "Goodness, I wouldn't dream of undertaking such a monumental feat," she said blithely, hoping he wouldn't pursue the subject. She should have known it wouldn't work.

"Don't try to sidestep me, girl. You're the first in some twenty-seven years to follow the law—at least on your granddad's side of the family. But you take on too much."

Shelby wanted to tell him he was wrong, but unfortunately he was dead right. With the exception of her father, none of Charles Delacroix's children had opted for a career in law. Her aunt Toni had chosen music, her uncle Remy...well, poor Remy had his own set of problems and favored his swamp-tour business over the family money. And Shelby was the only one of Charles's five grandchildren who had decided to become a lawyer. Her sister Charly had just graduated from the New Orleans Police Academy, but according to their grandfather, that hardly counted. Jax and Beau had found success, she with the Thoroughbreds and he with just making money at everything he did. Marie was...well, Marie—sweet, wonderful and, in Shelby's opinion, a bit of a ditz. Shelby was the only direct descendant of Charles Delacroix in the firm, since Justin had retired and taken the federal judgeship.

"I'm fine, Bear, and I didn't come to be scolded. I came to ride."

"At least you still have that much good sense left."

Tenacity was second nature to Bear, and Shelby could see she was in for a lecture if she stayed. "Think I'll say hi to Jax before I ride. Know where she is?"

"Down by the track."

Shelby left, annoyed at having to postpone her ride. She would come back after Bear left the stables.

When she got to the track, Jax was nowhere to be found, so she contented herself with watching the exercise boys put a couple of two-year-olds through their paces. It had rained the night before, and as the horses came around the turn where Shelby watched, she was forced to step back to avoid being splattered. She recognized one of the boys, Randy, on the inside, riding Takeachance, but the other exerciser, riding Arabesque on the side nearest the fence, she didn't recognize. He was undoubtedly new. And maybe a little green, she thought, noticing that every so often he struggled for control of Arabesque.

Even so, the sight of the healthy, well-trained Thoroughbreds flexing their sleek muscles as they breezed around the track was like watching art in motion. Flawless, powerful, they were truly a joy to behold. Feeling free and happy, she realized she had been away from the horses and riding for too long.

TRAVIS EXITED the Delacroix Farms office and headed toward the track, where Jax Delacroix had promised to meet him in a few moments. As he approached, he noticed a woman leaning against the fence. Just then a breeze ruffled her dark hair, and she turned her face to the wind and closed her eyes. He stopped and stared.

Travis had a respect and appreciation for natural beauty, instilled in him from childhood by his father. The grandeur of the land, his magnificent quarter horses, even the occasional turbulent and dramatic Hill Country weather often touched him deeply, and he found an overwhelming grace, beauty and power in all things natural. It had to do with being a part of nature, not just in it.

What Travis saw in this woman now was natural beauty. Not just a pretty face and a nice figure, although she had that and more; what caught his attention was the expression of joy on her face. Pure, natural joy. It was compelling and undeniably attractive. He couldn't remember the last time a woman had captivated him so completely. It was odd, maybe even a little corny, but he felt drawn to her—even to feeling that if he called to her she would turn to him with a smile, as if they already knew each other. When she turned her attention to the horses, he was disappointed.

He wondered who she was. Dressed in casual clothes, she probably wasn't a client of Delacroix Farms, but from the way she watched the horses he would bet she knew her way around the track. An employee? Whoever the woman was, she was just about the most enthralling creature he had ever seen. He had to meet her.

Shelby was so engrossed in her observation that she didn't hear footsteps until they were right behind her.

"Good-looking horses."

She turned to find a tall man in a cowboy hat watching the riders put the horses through their paces.

The brim of the hat shaded his face so that she couldn't see his eyes, but his voice was kind, friendly, and she noted a bit of drawl. "The best," she responded proudly. "But I guess I'm prejudiced."

He turned toward her. "You work here?"

*Wow,* Shelby thought, a little surprised at the immediate and powerful reaction she was having to a total stranger. *Handsome* was too pretty a word to apply to him. *Rugged* was better. *Appealing,* definitely. He had that Marlboro Man thing going for him, and it worked. She put her hand up to shade her eyes, hoping to get a better view of the stranger, and smiled. "I used to."

"Well—" he propped a booted foot on the bottom rail of the fence "—the Delacroix sure bred some fine animals."

"Absolutely." She wondered who he was. Obviously he wasn't from Bayou Beltane, because he didn't appear to know who she was. Most of the Delacroix were recognized for miles, which Shelby had discovered was both a blessing and a curse. The same could be said for her terminal curiosity, and at the moment she was dying to know more about this man. "Are you just admiring, or are you interested in buying?"

Travis looked her up and down, knowing the sun in her eyes worked to his advantage. "A little of both." Again he liked what he saw, especially the smile.

"Do you mind if I ask where you're from?"

"Now, why should I mind a pretty woman asking me anything?"

A charmer, Shelby thought. Well, a little charm was good for a lady's ego now and then. "I don't suppose you should, unless you're running from the law or an ex-wife. I might have a problem with the law, but you're on your own with the ex.''

Sass. He liked that, too. A natural dark-haired beauty with brains and killer gray eyes. She was something special. He pushed the brim of his hat back so she could see his face. ''No worries on that score, darlin'.''

''Let me guess. You're from Texas.''

''Bull's-eye. Ever heard of a place called Comfort?''

''The Hill Country. One of my favorite places in the state.''

Travis smiled. ''You've got good taste.''

It was slightly unnerving to have such dazzling male attention focused on her, but pleasant all the same. ''Do you, uh, do you own Thoroughbreds yourself?''

''Quarter horses. But I'm in the market for a brood mare with a good bloodline to enhance my stock.''

Shelby cocked her head and grinned. ''You know, I think this is the only business where you can still make a statement like that and not have a feminist riot on your hands.''

Travis threw his head back and laughed. ''Oh, but I do like a lady who speaks her mind.''

''Then, you're in luck,'' Shelby said, giving as good as she got.

''I decided that the minute I laid eyes on you.''

Her cheeks felt flushed, and she covered a tinge of nervousness with small talk. ''Is this a buying trip or just looking?''

''Reconnaissance. You sure do ask a lot of questions.''

Shelby hadn't realized she had been grilling him like a witness. "I'm sorry. That was rude of me. Please, accept my apology, Mr...."

"Hardin. Travis Hardin. And I prefer to think you were interested instead of rude."

She offered her hand. "Mr. Hardin—"

"I answer to Travis, darlin'." He didn't release her hand immediately.

Shelby recognized a smooth move when she saw one, and she had no doubt Travis Hardin was experienced in smooth moves. Still, she couldn't honestly say she was relieved when he released her hand. "Nice to meet you, Travis."

Make that a double wow, she thought, leaning against the fence rail. He might be smooth and experienced, but he was most certainly not boring.

"Same here, Ms....?"

"Oh, uh, Shelby—"

At that moment the horses came thundering around the track. Shelby glanced over her shoulder. Instantly she knew Arabesque was out of control and headed straight for the fence.

Travis turned at almost the same moment, realized what was about to happen and acted instinctively. A split second before the horse hit the rail Shelby was leaning against, he grabbed her around the waist and literally swept her off her feet and out of harm's way. The two riders reined the Thoroughbreds to a stop, dismounted and starting inspecting the animals for injury.

"You okay?" Travis asked, gazing down at the petite woman in his arms.

"I think so. But the horses..."

"Hey," Travis called to the riders. "Everybody in one piece?"

"He just blew the turn," the obviously more experienced hand answered. He patted the neck of the horse that had hit the rail. "A scratch or two, that's all."

"There you go, darlin'." Reluctantly, he set Shelby back on her feet. "One damsel rescued."

"Thanks to you."

"Anytime..." He nodded in the direction of the two exercise boys. "That kid's too green for a muddy track."

"He'll learn," she said, straightening her T-shirt, which seemed to have shifted off one shoulder as she was rescued. She stopped abruptly and looked at him. "I'd appreciate it if you didn't mention this to anyone. I'm sure the boy feels bad enough about what happened. I'd hate to see him get fired over this."

Looks, sass and a tender heart. Not a bad combination, Travis decided. "Pushover for underdogs, huh?"

Shelby shrugged. "Everybody deserves a second chance."

"All right. You got it."

"Well, thanks again for the rescue, and I hope you find just the brood mare you're looking for." Another breeze swirled past them and blew several strands of dark hair across her cheek.

Before he realized what he was doing, Travis brushed the hair from her cheek, tucking it behind her ear. "So far, darlin', it's been a real pleasure."

She didn't object. In fact, it felt as if he had just paid her a lovely compliment. "Well," she said barely above a whisper. "Goodbye." And she took off.

"Hold on a sec—"

"Mr. Hardin," someone called, and Travis turned to see another stable boy trying to get his attention. "Ms. Delacroix said to tell you... Never mind," he said. "Here she comes."

Travis looked back at the disappearing Shelby with No Last Name and reminded himself this trip was strictly business. He couldn't afford to get sidetracked. But that didn't stop a second glance and a pang of regret.

He started walking toward the barn and met Jax Delacroix halfway. "We can take a look at that mare now if you're ready," she said in greeting.

"Fine with me," he answered, turning to follow her. But his enthusiasm for looking at the mare had faded.

Jax and Travis had almost reached the stable entrance when a shiny, black, late-model Buick came down the lane, slowed, then stopped. The rear window came down. Jax smiled and waved.

"Travis," she said, "would like to meet my grandfather? He's the real heart of Delacroix Farms."

Travis couldn't believe his good luck. His first day in Bayou Beltane and he was about to meet the man he suspected of murder.

"Jax, I can't think of anything I'd like better."

# CHAPTER THREE

TRAVIS HADN'T EXPECTED this, wasn't really prepared for it, but here it was, nonetheless. His pulse hammered at his temples and adrenaline spurted through his veins as the driver got out and opened the rear door.

If Travis had been expecting the devil incarnate, he was disappointed. Even though he knew Delacroix was nearing eighty, he wasn't prepared to face an archetypal grandfather, complete with white hair and a golfing cardigan. Not to mention a genuine Southern drawl. The man couldn't have appeared less threatening.

"Granddad," Jax said, "this is Travis Hardin. Travis, my grandfather, Charles Delacroix."

"Mr. Delacroix." For a split second, Travis almost didn't extend his hand, but a lifetime of good manners tempered his frustration.

Charles smiled as they shook hands. "My granddaughter tells me you're interested in crossbreeding, Mr. Hardin."

"Yes, sir, I am." The old man's smile might have been soft, but his eyes were sharp and assessing. And from the way he gave him the once-over, from his costly Luchse boots to the equally expensive Resistol cowboy hat, Travis estimated Delacroix had him categorized and filed under new money and no class.

"Well, I hope we can accommodate you. At my age, I don't keep up with the day-to-day operations the way I used to, but I do try to keep up with what's going on in the business. Crossbreeding is a fascinating aspect. You breed quarter horses, I believe?"

"Yes, but I'm expanding my operation." Travis noticed that despite his age and harmless demeanor, Charles had a way of dominating a conversation. He also noticed that since introducing them, Jax Delacroix had definitely taken a back seat to her granddaddy. "I'm looking for a good mare to help me build a string of polo ponies," he continued.

"Polo ponies. Did you hear that, Jacqueline? Sounds like Mr. Hardin knows how to diversify. Maybe we should think along those lines."

"I'm, uh, planning on showing him Zaira," she said.

"Excellent. Zaira has produced some quality foals."

"Your granddaughter has given me a thorough appraisal. Very comprehensive, very professional." The compliment earned Travis a half smile from Jax.

"So, Mr. Hardin, you think there's a market for polo ponies, do you?"

"Yes, sir, I do." Despite the fact that he suspected Delacroix was responsible for murder and misery, the manners his grandmother had drilled into him refused to be denied. "Polo is an increasingly popular sport, particularly in the Southwest."

"All those wide-open spaces, I suppose."

"Probably."

"Well," Charles said, "I mustn't keep you. I'm sure you're anxious to take a look at Zaira, make your decision, then get back to your family in…San Antonio, is it?"

"Not far from there. But I'll be in town for a while."

"Splendid. Do enjoy your stay." Charles turned to Jax. "Jacqueline, when you've concluded your business with Mr. Hardin, would you come up to the house?"

"Of course, Granddad."

"Delighted to meet you, Mr. Hardin."

"Thank you." Travis shook his hand for the second and, he hoped, last time.

As he followed Jax toward the barn, he wondered what Delacroix must have been like as a young man. What had first attracted Camille to him? Travis had read enough about Charles to know that he was still considered one of the best legal minds in the state. In the corporate world, his law firm had an excellent reputation. In personal terms, he was known to be a ruthless but fair deal maker. Remembering the slightly condescending once-over Delacroix had given him, Travis wondered if he had decided poor, sweet Camille Gravier wasn't a good fit for the future he had planned. Maybe Delacroix had had bigger fish to fry, and Camille and her baby would have been an inconvenience he couldn't afford. Maybe in a heated moment he had—

"Travis?"

"Yes?" He'd been so deep in thought he hadn't realized they had entered the barn and were now at the mare's stall.

"Is everything all right?"

"Yeah. I'm just getting a headache." He rubbed the bridge of his nose. "All this humidity, I guess."

"Probably. Do you need something to take for it? In the office I've—"

"No, I'm okay. Let's see the mare."

Jax gave the nod, and a stable boy put a halter and lead shank on the horse, then led her into the paddock while they followed. Travis checked to be sure the mare had good confirmation, and that her legs were straight.

"She had a promising future until she bowed a tendon," Jax told him. "But you couldn't ask for a sweeter disposition." The mare nuzzled Jax. "Yeah, you're a real sweetheart, aren't you, baby. Zaira is the Gaelic form of Sara, which means 'princess.' And that's exactly what she is."

Travis didn't need to be told Jax loved horses; it was there in the glow on her face, in the way she handled the mare with both love and respect. He knew she was a world-class equestrian, but out of her granddaddy's shadow she was also a competent businesswoman. She was sophisticated, attractive and savvy. Under different circumstances, he might have been interested—current circumstances being that he had just met a certain dark-haired beauty with gray eyes that he couldn't put out of his mind. The more he tried not to think about Shelby, the more he thought of her. He couldn't remember the last time a woman had affected him so strongly, if ever. The attraction was physical, no doubt about it. But there was something else, something too powerful simply to be labeled *desire*. Then again, he had a feeling that nothing about his attraction to Shelby was simple.

"Your granddaddy mentioned she was a good producer," he said, trying to focus on business.

"Two of her foals have done very well at the track."

"How does she haul?"

"Travels like a dream." She patted the mare's smooth neck. "You're an easy hauler, aren't you, Zaira?"

"She looks good," Travis said. "Real good." Truthfully, the mare looked great. Buying stock was not just an excuse for coming to Bayou Beltane. He needed a mare and definitely planned a purchase, but not too quickly. Once the mare was ready to travel, he would be, too.

"Appreciate your time, Jax. The animal is well worth the price and would be an asset to any operation. I'm just not sure she's for me." At Jax's raised eyebrow, he said, "Don't go thinking this is a trick to get you to lower your price. I'll be around for almost a week, and I'm gonna look at several other mares."

"Of course. You should."

Travis patted Zaira's neck. "She's a dandy, no doubt about it."

"Thanks."

"How would it be if I give you a call in a couple of days?"

"That'll be fine. And Travis…"

"Yeah?"

"You can look all you want, but I think you'll find Delacroix Farms will be hard to beat."

Travis smiled. "Wouldn't doubt it a bit." He tipped his hat. "I'll probably be seeing you."

He had intended to return to his motel in Slidell after leaving Delacroix Farms, but changed his mind and drove into Bayou Beltane instead. He cruised the quaint little town, which was much like small towns everywhere. Travis told himself he was giving the town a look because he was curious, because he had time to kill and nowhere to kill it. Truthfully, he was hoping to see Shelby with No Last Name. After fifteen minutes, and a closer look at Bayou Beltane than he cared to have, he pulled his truck to a stop near a small city park. It was nearing sundown and he decided to find a place to eat. As he strolled past several shops he glanced inside, each time hoping to see a familiar smile and killer gray eyes. But no dice. *Get over it, cowboy. She's probably forgotten all about you by now.*

SHELBY WAS RESTLESS. Truthfully, she couldn't get Travis Hardin off her mind. *Attracted* didn't even begin to define her reaction to him. One thing was certain, feeling that first zing of real chemistry was almost as scary as it was exciting. Of course, attraction was one thing, a real relationship was another. And a sexual relationship was a whole other ball game.

Over the last three years, she had spent a lot of time wondering what would happen when she felt "it" again. Falling in love and having sex might not matter so much if Shelby didn't know herself so well. Her passions ran deep, and when she fell in love—as with everything else she did—she committed herself all the way. No holding back. But she had also learned that loving someone didn't automatically make him a good person.

Or trustworthy.

One thing she had learned from her disastrous love affair and from therapy was that she could trust her own instincts. After all, the first time she'd met Royce

Baker, shortly after starting her third year of law school, her instincts had warned her that he was too good to be true. But she had been looking for a knight in shining armor—a foolish young girl's dream, perhaps, but true. And Royce was so bright, so utterly charming, that she ignored the warning and responded with her heart. And fell like the proverbial ton of bricks.

Looking back on that time now, Shelby found it hard to believe she had been so gullible. Even harder to believe was the fact that she hadn't seen through Royce's thin veneer of brash self-confidence to the truly selfish person beneath. But she had loved him so much she'd seen what she wanted to, missing the fact that selfishness often includes a mean streak.

Her knight had turned out to be anything but honorable.

She had learned a bitter lesson about love and self-preservation. But while Shelby might have been down, she never stayed down for long. Now that she knew her weakness, she knew what to guard against. If she had one character flaw, it was that she felt too much, too deeply. It was one of the traits that made her a good lawyer, but it was also a dangerous pitfall when it came to being objective about romance. Yet despite everything that had happened, she believed that the knight of her dreams still existed. Somewhere out there was an honorable man for her, and she had two advantages: she had a naturally sunny disposition, and she knew what she wanted and wasn't willing to settle for less. Simply put, she wanted what her aunt Toni and Brody had. And after meeting Travis Hardin, she was feeling better about the possibility of getting it.

Just thinking about Travis brought his image to mind. He certainly was appealing. So was the idea of running into him again. Actually, it was tantalizing. Deliciously tantalizing. Shelby savored the thought as she drove her little convertible back into Bayou Beltane, the October sun sliding toward the horizon like a big orange ball rolling toward tomorrow.

This was her favorite time of day—sunlight barely hanging on while the night crept closer. The air was heavy with the scent of wildflowers blooming along the road, and dusk was beginning to form shadows the night would complete. She could almost see the heat of the day slowly softening, slowly being seduced by sultry darkness.

Shelby parked her car a couple of doors down from the Catholic church and walked across the street to the Snowcone Stand. Waiting in line, she glanced around and caught sight of the man who had occupied her thoughts steadily for the last few hours. Travis Hardin. Perched on one of the wooden benches in the small park directly across from the church, he was eating a snowcone. He stood up and waved.

Shelby waved back, telling herself she should probably go over and speak to him, just to be polite. She was one of the few people he had met in town, so of course he would be friendly, and expect her to be. After all, it was only good manners. Oh, who was she kidding? The idea of *not* joining him never crossed her mind. She turned her attention to the small lineup, and didn't notice that Travis was approaching the stand.

"Hey there," he said as she stepped up to place her order.

"Hi."

He held up his half-eaten snowcone. "I can recommend the Very Cherry."

"I think I'm in the mood for—" she surveyed the list of flavors "—Radical Raspberry."

He raised an eyebrow. "Daring. Very daring."

"Hey, what's life without a little danger?" She paid for her snowcone, and they strolled toward the park.

"Figured you'd had enough for one day."

Shelby just laughed.

"Can't tell you how glad I am to see you've got a sweet tooth."

"Why?"

"If you hadn't come looking for Radical Raspberry, I'd be sitting here all alone." He leaned a little closer. "And I was sure hoping to see you again."

"Were you?" She might be a bit rusty when it came to this kind of close-encounter flirting, but she hoped it was like learning to ride a bicycle—once you got the hang of it, you never really forgot. "Did you buy a mare from Delacroix Farms?"

Travis was so engrossed in watching her lick stray ice crystals he barely heard her. "I looked at an eight-year-old named Zaira."

"Great choice. She's a good producer."

When she held the snowcone to her mouth, it wasn't hard for his imagination to leap to some very erotic images. He cleared his throat. "I'm still looking."

"Delacroix Farms will be hard to beat."

"Yeah, but I like to take my time." He took a bite of his own snowcone. "So, uh, tell me. What do you do around here for entertainment and good food?"

"Drive to Slidell."

Travis laughed. "Darlin', I just came from there. Other than my motel and a couple of fast-food places, it's more or less limited."

"You could always drive to New Orleans." She wondered just what he meant by "limited." Somehow she couldn't picture him as a party animal, but... "There are a lot of clubs—"

"I'm not looking for a pick-up joint." He tossed the last of his soggy paper cone into a nearby trash bin, then stretched out his long legs and crossed his ankles. "I'm looking for a decent steak."

"Oh, well..." Shelby said, pleased with his answer. She crunched into her frozen treat, dislodging a chunk of ice and catching it with her tongue.

He should look away, Travis warned himself, but he didn't. Everything about this woman intrigued him, attracted him. "And some good company. You haven't, by any chance, already had dinner?"

"Is that an invitation?"

"You always answer a question with a question?"

"Sorry, force of habit. No, I haven't eaten." She held up her snowcone. "Thought I'd start with dessert first."

Thinking about food was a much-needed distraction at the moment. Every time Travis looked at Shelby's mouth he wanted to kiss her. Hell, he wanted to do more than kiss her. *Food, cowboy, food.* "About that steak. Please don't tell me you're a vegetarian."

"Far from it, but around here I'm afraid you're out of luck with the steak. Where do you stand on the issue of pan-fried catfish?"

"It's got my vote."

"There's a place down by the lake called the Catfish Shack. Now, I have to warn you the name is appropriate. It looks as if it's about to fall down, but you won't find better catfish within a hundred miles.''

"Sold." He stood up, took her snowcone and tossed it into the nearby trash container. "Let's go."

"Hey, I wasn't through with that."

"Darlin', I'll buy you another dessert. I'll buy you a dozen, if you'll just guide me to some decent food."

Shelby smiled. "Would you like to take my car? The top is down."

Travis grinned. "You're reading my mind." He grabbed her hand. "Which way?"

THE CATFISH SHACK wasn't a tourist kind of place, but it did boast outdoor dining. If you liked redwood picnic tables, that is. Nor did it clutter customers' minds with an extensive menu, or a menu at all, for that matter. The owners served catfish, french fries and beer, family style. They had obviously decided anything else was overkill, in the same way they'd decided waiters were unnecessary. Orders were placed and picked up at the window.

"As much as I like a good, thick steak," Travis said, after polishing off his fifth or sixth fillet, "this is the best food I've had in weeks."

"Don't they feed cowboys in Texas?" Shelby asked, pushing her plate away. "Or are you forced to eat your own cooking?"

Travis finished another fillet. "Gran used to cook for my dad and me."

"Used to?"

"She…passed on recently."

"Travis, I'm so sorry." Reacting instinctively, Shelby touched his hand.

It was a small gesture, but it moved him deeply.

He had never felt such an immediate and powerful connection to a woman the way he did with Shelby. It was both strangely comforting and unsettling at the same time. "It's been the three of us since my mom died when I was a kid, so it's kinda hard to make the adjustment."

"Sounds like she was very important to you."

"Yeah," he said, "just about the most important person in the world."

"My mother left when I was seventeen. Not that divorce can compare to death." The shrug of Shelby's narrow shoulders might have been intended as nonchalant, but he saw her pain. Recognized a fellow survivor. Maybe that was the connection he had felt. Whatever it was, he didn't want it to end. "I know that losing someone close is difficult," she added.

"Thanks." He eyed the last piece of catfish in the basket, both because the meal was delicious and because he wanted to change the subject. "If you're not going to eat that, I think it's calling my name."

"Brother, you really are a glutton for punishment. Go for it. If I ever get to Texas, I'll expect equal treatment with barbecue ribs."

Travis looked into her eyes. "Darlin', you name the day. Nothing would please me more than to show you around personally."

His gaze was so intense, Shelby felt her skin actually grow warm. Images of Travis holding her to him danced through her mind. "I, uh, better warn you, I've been known to embarrass myself when it comes to consuming ribs."

"I'll take you to Cooper's. Kinda like this." He gestured toward the weathered shack. "Not much on atmosphere, but the beef and pork are so tender, the meat falls right off the bone and melts in your mouth.''

''Hmm. Sounds like my kind of place.''

He polished off the last of the catfish and wiped his face and hands. ''Now, I believe I owe you dessert. Didn't I hear the guy at the window mention fried apple pie?''

''Probably deep-fried, then dipped in a sugar glaze.''

Travis patted his stomach. ''Hmm. I love it when you talk fat grams. Let's order two pieces.''

''You're tempting me.''

Again he looked straight into her eyes. ''That's the whole point, darlin'.''

Exactly when they had ceased talking about pie, she wasn't sure, but the conversation had definitely taken a more personal turn. ''Maybe I should stick to what I know is good for me.''

''Possibly. But it's a whole lot more fun when you don't. Besides, you don't strike me as a strictly-by-the-rules kind of woman.''

''Oh, but I am.'' Shelby smiled. ''Particularly when they're my rules.''

He leaned across the table. ''You are direct, aren't you?''

''Afraid so.''

''Well, I can't argue with that. I usually play by my own rules, too.'' He leaned back. ''So what's it gonna be? Indulge or deny yourself?''

''Indulge…moderately.''

After Travis devoured his pie and Shelby consumed only half of hers, they drove back into town. By the time they reached the park, darkness had fallen and the landscape lights were on, illuminating the walkways with soft dots of light. Only a few shops were still open, and for the most part everyone had left "downtown" Bayou Beltane.

"Not much happens here after dark," Shelby commented. "At least not in public."

"Yeah. It's the same in Comfort."

"Not that it prevents people from talking about everything that does happen, and embellishing as they go."

"Gossip and small towns are joined at the hip."

"I suppose. For instance, by tomorrow morning, you and I will be the topic of conversation over everyone's coffee. The fact that no one knows who you are will only add fuel to the gossip flames. I wouldn't be surprised, by the time they're finished, to hear that you and I were making mad, passionate love on this bench."

"And you wouldn't like that."

"What? Being gossiped about—"

"Making mad, passionate love with me."

Shelby's heart hammered against her rib cage, and for a second she held her breath. "You're pretty direct yourself."

"Didn't mean to throw you for a loop, but I didn't figure there was any use lying to you. You know I'm attracted to you. And before you say anything, let me add that if you're not interested, I'll deal with it. My ego isn't so fragile that I can't stand rejection."

"I—I'd be lying if I said I wasn't attracted to you. I'm just not sure what to do about it. My instincts tell me one thing, my common sense another."

"A little common sense is good, but sometimes instincts are too strong to ignore. What do yours tell you?"

"Oh, brother," Shelby said, a little nervously. She wasn't sure if that was from caution or excitement. "I'm not certain you want to know."

"Yeah, I do. If you followed those instincts right now, what would happen?"

"Well…" Her smile vanished, and in the glow from the lights her eyes softened. "I—I guess I'd kiss you."

The hard kick of desire was like a blow to his gut. He wanted to haul her into his arms and let both of their instincts go wild, but the word *guess* stopped him. Maybe she'd been hurt. From all appearances she looked like a real together lady, but then, broken hearts were invisible to the naked eye. Unexpectedly, he felt a powerful need to protect her from anything that might cause her a moment's discomfort.

Travis smiled. "Not that I wouldn't enjoy every minute, darlin', but I think we'd better wait until you're sure." He took a step back.

The instant he moved away, Shelby knew exactly what she wanted. She reached out and touched his arm. "I'm sure."

There was nothing tentative about her kiss. It was warm, seductive and certain. And there was certainly nothing tentative about the way Travis responded. Before she realized what was happening, he was in control, kissing her deeply. If there had been even half a heartbeat of hesitation, it was lost in the glow of feeling secure in his embrace. She wound her arms around his neck and kissed him back. Thoroughly.

Travis knew the instant she crossed the line, stepping past caution and into passion. Whatever had caused the hesitation was gone, and he was reaping the benefits. Angling his mouth over hers, he deepened the kiss, wishing they were someplace more private.

His mouth feasted on hers, greedy for more. And she offered more, straining as if she needed to experience all the desire, all at once. Then slowly, the first demanding rush slipped into a softer, more seductive kiss.

An aching pleasure glided through her, so sweet, so welcome it made her want to cry. This was what she had been afraid she had lost forever. This was the healing balm for the pain that had gone before. Shelby gloried in her return to the realm of exquisitely delicious sensations only passion provided. But more than that, she welcomed feeling so secure in Travis's arms.

Travis held her to him, enjoying the feel of her body pressed to his. While part of him wanted nothing more than to go on kissing her for hours, the reality of where they were made that impractical. Slowly, regretfully, he ended the kiss. When she drew back, her face was flushed, her eyes dreamy. He slipped a hand to the back of her neck, and his thumb coasted across her lips. "God, you're sweet."

"That was…wonderful," she whispered. "You're wonderful."

He smiled and kissed her soft mouth once more. But he didn't linger. He didn't dare.

"I know you're only going to be, uh…" She tried to find words to tell him she wanted to see him but didn't expect anything from him. "What I mean is that I'd like to see you again while you're in town. However long that will be."

He slipped an arm around her waist, and they walked the few yards to her car. "You're reading my mind again."

"Will you call me?" she asked, standing beside the convertible.

"I'd love to, darlin', but who should I ask for? Miss Shelby with No Last Name?"

Shelby's mouth dropped open. "Oh, my Lord. I was introducing myself when Arabesque slammed into the... Oh, Travis. What must you think of me? I just kissed you in a public park, and I haven't even bothered to give you my last name."

"Do you see me complaining?"

"Well..." She reached inside her purse and retrieved a business card. "Obviously, your manners are better than mine."

"Darlin', sometimes names and manners aren't priorities when you meet someone who interests you."

"Yes," she said, surprised and more than a little thrilled to see desire still sparking in his eyes. "This was the best time I've had in...I can't remember when."

"Same here. You're good company."

"Thanks. So are you."

He took the card. "Good night."

"Good night, Travis," she said, sliding into the convertible. She waved as she drove off.

Travis watched her until she drove out of sight. He felt good—in fact, better than he had in weeks. He glanced at the card she had given him, a wide smile plastered on his face.

For a moment, he thought his mind was playing tricks on him, but it wasn't.

The card read Shelby Delacroix, Attorney-at-Law, Delacroix and Associates.

## CHAPTER FOUR

TRAVIS COULDN'T STOP staring at the card, his mind grappling with the printed words. He saw them, but he didn't believe them. Yet there they were in black and white.

Shelby Delacroix, Attorney-at-Law.

She was a *Delacroix!*

Bits and pieces of their conversation flooded his memory. When he'd asked her if she worked at the farm, she'd said, "I used to."

And when he met her at the park... "Did you buy a horse from Delacroix Farms? Great choice. She's a good producer."

Then again, before they went to dinner, he'd asked her if she always answered a question with a question, and she'd responded, "Sorry, force of habit."

She had given him clues to her identity all along. How could he have missed the obvious?

Because his judgment had been clouded by testosterone and some fantasy, that's why.

As Travis walked to his truck, got in and headed for Slidell, he cursed himself for a fool ten times over. He had wanted Shelby from the minute he laid eyes on her, and he'd had a helluva time keeping his mind on business.

*My God,* he thought, zipping along the highway well past the speed limit. *I kissed her.*

No. She had kissed him.

*But I didn't exactly push her away.*

As much as he wanted to blame Shelby, the truth was that he'd been so into kissing her he probably wouldn't have cared what her last name was. Even now, just thinking about how she tasted, how she felt in his arms, had him aroused. How the hell was he supposed to deal with this—this complication? he wondered as he pulled into the motel parking lot and braked to a stop outside his room.

There was only one way.

He would just have to stay the hell away from Shelby.

What else could he do? She must be Charles Delacroix's granddaughter, for Pete's sake. Bayou Beltane was a small town with an active grapevine, and people had seen them together. Hell, that kiss would probably make the front page of the newspaper. Travis couldn't go openly poking around in the past after being seen with her. It was bound to get back to Shelby. No, he had to stay away from her.

He got out of his truck and slammed the door, wanting to swing at something. The truth was the thought of walking away from Shelby was more distasteful than the knowledge that she was Charles Delacroix's granddaughter. It shouldn't have been, but it was. Travis couldn't get the image of her as he'd first seen her out of his mind. So sweet and sassy. And refreshingly honest. He remembered the joy on her face, the softness of her cheek....

*Whoa, cowboy. This is no good.*

Once inside his room, Travis made straight for the phone. He needed to talk to his dad.

"Hey, Trav," T.C. said the minute he heard his son's voice. "Been hopin' you'd call."

"How's everything going?"

"Fine. Maggie had her litter of pups. Eleven of 'em. She's short a couple of spigots, so we're hand-feedin' the runts. How's it with you?"

"Okay. Dad, did the private detective call?"

"Foster, right? Nope, not a peep."

"Well, I met Charles Delacroix."

T.C.'s long, low whistle almost hurt Travis's ear. "You didn't waste no time. What's he like?"

"'Bout what we expected." After a long pause, Travis added, "I spoke to Jax Delacroix about business, but I also met another granddaughter."

"Well, since the tone of your voice just changed, I figure that presents some kind of problem, right? What happened? She find out who you are?"

"No. In fact, I think it's possible she doesn't even know what happened back in 1938."

"You sound mighty certain."

"Just a hunch."

"Well, that might work to your advantage. If she don't know, you could question her about her family's past and she might give you information without even realizin' it."

Use Shelby? Pump her for information that they could use against her granddaddy? That's what his dad was talking about. The whole idea made Travis wince.

"Folks might feel a little more like loosenin' their tongues if she was with you."

Every instinct Travis possessed was telling him the chances that Shelby knew about her granddaddy's involvement with Camille's murder were slim. Or was that just wishful thinking? Maybe. Probably. All he knew was the thought of involving her left a bitter taste in his mouth. And the only way to avoid that was to avoid her.

"That's pretty cold, Dad."

"What they did to your great-aunt was pretty damn cold. No tellin' what this granddaughter might reveal in the right situation."

The right situation? Travis thought. Like cozy dinners, sweet talk and kisses under the trees? Suddenly he realized meeting Shelby was both a curse and a blessing. He didn't like the idea of using her. He'd never experienced such an instant connection with anyone as he had with Shelby, but he couldn't pretend he'd come to town for fun and games. He was here to find the truth. Nothing else should matter.

"You still there, Trav?"

"Yeah. You're right. If she can provide me with information, so much the better."

"Why, sure. A little sweet talk can go a long way."

"Yeah. Well, I better let you go. If Foster calls, give him my number here."

"All right, son. Take care."

"You, too," Travis said, and hung up. He stretched out on the bed and gazed at the ceiling.

He didn't like it, but he'd do it. He'd sweet talk Shelby Delacroix. He'd pay her compliments, kiss her and be so damn charming that she couldn't resist him. He'd do whatever it took, even if that meant…what? Sleeping with her?

Travis closed his eyes and tried to recall Gran's face, but for the first time ever, he couldn't. What disturbed him even more was that the image that quickly came to mind was Shelby. *Would* he make love to her in order to accomplish his revenge?

Too many questions and not enough answers, he decided as he got off the bed and headed for a hot shower. Too much had happened today. Not the least of which was finding a woman he thought special, only to discover she was blood kin to the man he was certain murdered his great-aunt.

Nothing felt right. Nothing was turning out as he had expected. Only one thing was certain: he wished Shelby's last name had been Smith.

WHEN SHELBY AWOKE, she was as restless as she had been the night before, and for the same reason: Travis Hardin. She couldn't get him off her mind. Last night had been a real coming out for her, and it was all because of Travis. All because she had gone with her instinct to trust him. And just look what had happened.

While she dressed, then drove to work, she kept remembering the feel of his mouth on hers, the joy of being held in his arms. She was so engrossed in her thoughts that by the time she made it to the office she wasn't even aware she was humming "Happy Days Are Here Again." She practically waltzed into the break room.

"My, aren't we chipper this morning," said Joanna Delacroix Gideon as she opened the door to the microwave and removed the healthful, homemade bran muffin she had just finished heating.

"Yes, we are. The sun is shining, the birds are singing and all is right with the world."

Joanna held up the muffin. "Care to split this with me?"

"No, thanks. I'm not hungry."

"Hmm." Joanna set the muffin aside and poured a cup of coffee. "Sounds suspicious, if you ask me. Loss of appetite, a ridiculously optimistic view of the world, and not even the vitamin therapy I've recommended to help account for these symptoms. If I had to draw a conclusion, I would say romance might be a probable cause."

Shelby went very still. "Romance? Whatever gave you that idea? I never mentioned a word about any man—"

"Ah, I rest my case. The witness has indicted herself. Can I assume this means you've met someone?"

"Well…"

"Shelby, you're blushing." Seeing her cousin's reaction, Joanna hurried to apologize. "I'm sorry if I embarrassed you. I certainly never meant—"

"It's okay. Besides, you're right."

Shelby knew Joanna would never poke fun at any serious relationship—a statement she couldn't have made six months ago. Until Joanna had left her father's firm and come to work at Delacroix and Associates, Shelby hadn't really gotten to know her. Now Joanna was everything Shelby wanted to be— sophisticated, brilliant, scrupulously honest and an outstanding litigator. Despite the more than ten years' difference in their ages, they had become good friends. In fact, for the most part, Shelby felt closer to Joanna than she did to her own sisters.

Not that her sisters weren't dear to her—they were. She saw Charly and Marie often, but Jax had been gone for several years, and though they got along, they weren't close. Hopefully, now that she was back home for good, that would change. Even if it did,

Shelby knew her relationship with Joanna would always be special.

"Suspicions confirmed. What's his name? What does he do?" Joanna smiled. "And just how handsome is he?"

"Well, I didn't plan on being in the witness box, but... Travis Hardin. A rancher from Texas. And drop-dead gorgeous."

"Sounds like he's got potential."

Shelby grinned. "Definitely."

"You know," Joanna said in her usual serious tone, "I've been a little worried about you. I mean, you're a beautiful, smart—way too smart for most of the men in this town—young woman. You have all the social graces, yet you rarely date anyone more than once, and you only ever go to those awful bar association functions. I really was worried that you had decided to marry your career."

"What is this? A conspiracy? First Toni's worried about my love life, now you. Well, relax. You don't have to worry anymore."

"I'm happy for you. Believe me, I've been loved and I've been alone." Joanna glanced away. "Loved is better."

Shelby knew her cousin was remembering her late husband and the contented life they had shared until his death. Perhaps, Shelby thought, that was the reason she and Joanna had bonded so well and quickly. They shared the common ground of pain. Of course, Joanna knew nothing of what had happened with Royce, but still she seemed to sense an understanding.

"So, when do we get a look at this Prince Charming?"

"I don't even know if he'll call, and he's not going to be in town for long."

"I've just listed a few of your sterling qualities, so why wouldn't he call? And as for time, well…" Joanna shrugged. "If this turns out to be—pardon the expression—a hot and heavy relationship, Texas isn't exactly the other side of the world, you know."

Shelby frowned. "But what if he doesn't call?"

Joanna shook her head. "Am I ever glad I'm past the time in my life when I have to deal with all the insecurities that accompany youth."

"Like you're old."

"Totally ancient. Just ask Nikki."

"How is Nikki?" Shelby asked. "I haven't seen her in a while."

Shelby didn't miss the sudden shadow that shifted through her cousin's eyes. Her daughter was never an easy topic for Joanna to discuss. Shelby sensed there were serious problems there, but Joanna was too private a person to discuss them in any more than a superficial way.

"Nikki is sixteen, Shelby. And far too good at it. When you rope that cowboy of yours and have some kids, get them to skip the teenage years."

"I remember being sixteen," Shelby said, sensing the sudden strain in the conversation and wanting to ease it. "Nothing but raging hormones, zits and hard rock. I know I drove my dad crazy. But I outgrew it. Finally. So there's hope. If I can make it through, Nikki can."

Joanna looked at her and smiled. "You never fail to cheer me up, Shelby. I'm glad we're family."

"Same goes for me."

"And speaking of family," Joanna said, pouring

more coffee, "I talked to my sister, Annabelle, last night."

"Oh, how is she?"

"Separated."

"What?"

Joanna nodded solemnly. "She and Neal have called it quits. For good this time."

"I'm sorry, Joanna."

"I'm not. She's been miserable for the last two years. Ever since Cade broke his leg in that accident. He lost so much blood and they..."

"They what?"

Joanna frowned, as if searching for the right word, then sighed. "Oh, they...she and Neal just didn't turn to each other. I guess the crisis was the test point, and they both failed. Anyway, she and Cade are moving back to Bayou Beltane."

Again Shelby sensed there was more to the story than what Joanna was sharing, but she didn't push. "And what does your dad think about it?"

"Well, since he's not speaking to me these days, I can only go by what Annabelle says, and she told me that he's thrown out the welcome mat." Joanna glanced away.

"She's upset because you came to work with us, isn't she?" Shelby said.

"She thinks I've abandoned Dad—"

"She hasn't seen the side of Uncle Philip that you have."

"I doubt seriously that it would make any difference. Annabelle has always been Daddy's staunchest defender. As far as she's concerned, he's her knight in shining armor."

"With rusty hinges," Shelby muttered, then glanced at her cousin. "Sorry."

Joanna shook her head. "It's okay. I have very few illusions left where my father is concerned. Truthfully, my biggest regret is that it took me almost a year to see his machinations for what they were." She glanced away. "I may not approve of the way he does business, but he's still my father."

"What does Drew say about all of this?"

Joanna looked disgusted. "My brother is very busy trying to pattern his life after Dad's. As far as Drew is concerned, everything is status quo."

"You know, I hate to sound like a tattletale, but I ran into Drew in New Orleans a few weeks ago while I was having lunch with a girl I knew in college. He must have had a rough day. It was barely two in the afternoon and he was drinking pretty heavily."

"Doesn't surprise me. I hate it, but it doesn't surprise me."

"Well, it's a shame—"

The intercom buzzed. "Shelby, you have a call on line two."

"Shelby Delacroix," she announced when she picked up the phone.

"Good morning."

"Travis," she said, her voice between a whisper and a sigh. Joanna grinned, waved and left her alone to talk.

"It's not too early to call, is it?" He reminded himself that no matter how sweet she sounded, he hadn't come to Bayou Beltane for sweet talk. *Focus, cowboy, focus.*

"No. I was hoping…that is, I'm glad you called."

"Music to my ears, darlin'. You free for lunch?"

"Oh, I think that can be arranged."

"Since I'm a stranger in these parts, I'll let you suggest the place."

"As long as we don't go back to the Catfish Shack. I think it'll be a while before I'm compelled to make a return visit."

"Got a good, old-fashioned greasy hamburger joint around here?"

"And the optimum word there is *greasy,* right? I've got a place that's right up your alley, and not far from my office. Rick's Café."

"Sounds good to me. Eleven-thirty a good time for you?"

"It's fine."

"Want me to pick you up at your office or—" Travis dropped his voice "—we could meet at the park."

*Oh, my,* she thought. His voice was so sexy. "The, uh, the park, I think."

There was a slight pause before he said, "I'm looking forward to it, darlin'," and hung up.

Shelby sat unmoving for a long moment, her hand still resting on the phone, anticipation tingling through her body. If she wasn't careful, she could go for Travis in a big way. It was wonderful to know she was finally open to romance again, but she didn't want to tumble too fast. The responsible, mature thing to do was to get to know someone thoroughly. If she had taken more time to get to know Royce Baker, she might have suspected he was a control freak of the worst kind. Or would she have? Maybe passion had been more important than experiencing a real and lasting love. The problem was that she didn't know any other way to love but passionately, with her whole heart, body and soul. Just as she didn't know any other way to practice law.

With a wistful sigh, Shelby realized she didn't feel much like practicing law today. She glanced at the clock. Nine-thirty. At this rate, the morning was going to drag by like the last float in a parade. She rose, went to her office and attacked a pile of research notes for a case Joanna was preparing. The case was interesting, but Shelby's eyes continually strayed to her watch. At a quarter after eleven she couldn't stand it and called the receptionist to say she was going to lunch. She knew she would be early, but she didn't care. All that responsibility and maturity she was trying to develop couldn't compete with the thrill of seeing Travis again.

TRAVIS SPOTTED HER the minute he turned the corner nearest the park. She was waiting for him, and he should have been pleased. She had that same look of joy on her face that had first attracted him, and guilt stabbed his conscience. He supposed he should be glad that her eagerness would work right into his plan. And if he was careful about what he said, he wouldn't really have to lie and string her along.

*Who you trying to convince, cowboy?*

All right, so he was trying to convince himself. This wasn't going to be easy or fun.

"Hey there," Travis said as he approached her.

"Hey there, yourself." She had regretted getting to the park a few minutes early. It had given her too much time to speculate on whether or not he would be as attracted to her as he'd seemed last night. Had he decided she was just a pleasant, out-of-town diversion, or was he really interested in her? Would he pretend the kiss had never happened, or would they sort of pick up where they'd left off? What would she do if he ignored the kiss? What would she do if he didn't?

Shelby had almost made herself crazy with questions. In the end, she'd decided that if he chose to ignore the kiss, then she would follow his lead. After all, she had practically thrown herself at the man already. If he backed off... Well, truthfully, it wasn't what she hoped for, but her heart was still intact. She would survive.

Travis walked straight to her and gave her a quick kiss. "Ready?"

"Ready," she said.

As he slipped an arm around her waist, she realized she'd worried needlessly. She couldn't remember ever feeling this comfortable with a man. With anyone, for that matter. What was it about Travis that made her feel she could trust him? The way his gaze met hers directly? The deep pride she heard in his voice when he talked about his home, his father? Maybe it was the love in his eyes when he spoke of his late grandmother. Whatever it was, she wanted to enjoy it, not question it.

An hour later, inside Rick's Café, they were almost finished with their grilled hamburgers and mounds of french fries when Travis announced, "Think I'll poke around your little town this afternoon. All the history around here appeals to me."

"Really? I love history."

"Don't suppose you'd like to hire on as my personal guide?"

"I've got a mile-high stack of research that I have to tackle," she said. "Sorry, I wish I could."

"No sweat."

"Did you have someplace special in mind?"

He shook his head. "Some of my dad's people came from Louisiana several generations back."

"Were they French?"

"German. Thought I might try to see if any of their names popped up in any old records."

"What was their name?

"Schmidt," he lied. "I know it's the equivalent of tracking someone named Smith, but I figure, what the hell. I've got to look at another mare this afternoon, but I have some time on my hands."

"Well, the local library is pitifully inadequate, but you could start there. It's about a block and a half from the park, across the street from the elementary school."

"Sounds like a plan."

She watched him finish the last of his hamburger and tried to think of some cool, clever way of letting him know she wanted to see him tonight. Everything she came up with sounded too pushy, too desperate.

"Guess your family has lived around here a long time, haven't they," he said.

"There've been Delacroix in St. Tammany Parish for over a hundred and thirty years."

"Talk about roots. Must be a passel of Delacroix by now. I'm surprised there's not a street named after your family."

"Oh, there is. Down by the old depot. And you're right. There's a herd of us. On both sides."

"Both sides?"

"Our family has two branches. My grandfather and my great-uncle Philip had a falling out years ago, and we sort of split."

"Too bad," Travis murmured, hoping she would say more. "Family is important."

"Yes, it is. Frankly, I've never understood why the two brothers—twins, actually—haven't been willing to reconcile. Whatever happened must have been traumatic, because they haven't spoken to each other except when it was required by family business in almost sixty years, apparently."

The mention of the time frame made Travis's heart rate jump. "Maybe they're both so stubborn neither wants to be the first to bridge the gap."

"Now, that is a distinct possibility. You wouldn't believe how obstinate those two men can be. Even at seventy-nine, Granddad can still make a jury squirm. And Great-uncle Philip is a real piece of work. He's been a state senator for years, and I wouldn't even attempt to estimate how much power he has, or how he uses it."

Listening to Shelby talk, Travis felt as if he were peeking in the window of the family mansion, overhearing a private conversation. He was grateful for the information and ashamed of how he was getting it at the same time. His instincts told him that she knew very little, if anything, about her grandfather's past. But what if his instincts were wrong?

"You must think I'm terrible talking about my family like this. I didn't mean to make it sound as though we're in the middle of a Hatfields-and-McCoys-style feud. Actually, I have strong feelings about family loyalty."

"We've got that in common."

"The Delacroix are not always an admirable lot, but blood really is thicker than water. I don't know." She shrugged. "Maybe it's all tied up with my love of history, but your family is both your past and your future, and I believe you should stick by them no matter what.''

She couldn't have defined her position more clearly. Obviously, Shelby's loyalties were strong, maybe even unshakable. Disappointment nagged at Travis like a pouting child. Somewhere in the back of his mind, he had nurtured a hope that she might be objective where her granddaddy was concerned.

And the only reason for such hope was that he already cared more about her than he should.

As much as he tried to dismiss that idea, it refused to budge. *Get over it,* Travis told himself. *Get on with what you came for.*

''So, tell me, darlin'. Think you could pry yourself away from your family long enough to drive to New Orleans this evening?''

''New Orleans?''

''I took the liberty of making reservations at Commander's Palace, hoping you'd come with me.''

''Thank goodness,'' she exclaimed with a laugh.

''What's so funny?''

''I was just trying to think of a clever way to get you to ask me out. Which only goes to prove the old adage that honesty is the best policy. I should have just asked *you* out.''

''Like I said, I do fancy a lady who knows her own mind,'' he told her, trying to ignore the way her comment about honesty was punching his guilt button.

''I like you, Travis,'' Shelby said straight out.

''Same here, darlin'.'' Gazing into her lovely eyes, Travis wished he had the luxury to be as straightforward with her as she was with him. But even more, he wished he didn't have to feel guilty for meaning it.

Shelby gave him directions to Riverwood, and they made plans for Travis to pick her up at six o'clock. Then, with a wave, she strolled off toward her office. He watched her walk away, thinking the sooner he got back to Texas, the better he would feel. He shoved his hands deep into his pockets and headed for the library.

A half hour later he decided Shelby had been dead right when she had described the Bayou Beltane Public Library as "pitiful." There was little for him to find, so he decided his next stop would be the local newspaper.

In order to keep gossip to a minimum, Travis told the young man working there that he was a writer researching famous murder cases. He had run across a smattering of information about the Gravier murder case and wondered if they had a morgue. Unfortunately, many of the old files had been stored in a warehouse that had burned down about twenty years earlier, so Travis walked away empty-handed except for a tip. The young man had suggested that he make a trip to Covington, since it was the seat of government for the parish. They would probably have all the records he wanted.

Covington was twenty or thirty minutes away, and Travis doubted he would have much time to search and get back for his date with Shelby. *Tomorrow,* he thought. *Tomorrow morning, first thing.* In the meantime, he decided to snoop around. If he got lucky, he might find a talkative shopkeeper. If Bayou Beltane was as much like Comfort, Texas, as he suspected, there were undoubtedly a few folks around who loved to talk about the good old days. Travis was in the mood to listen.

SMILING TO HERSELF as she approached the offices of Delacroix and Associates, Shelby was so preoccupied that at first she didn't see the woman waving at her. When she did, it took her a moment to recognize her.

"Yvette," Shelby finally called out, waving back. Before the woman could start across the street, Shelby hurried over and embraced her. "Yvette! It is you. I'm so glad to see you. How've you been?"

"Just fine, Shelby." Nervously, Yvette glanced around. "How you doin'?"

"I'm doing great, thanks." If Yvette Avenall was supposed to be the picture of "fine," Shelby hated to think what "not so good" looked like. Once beautiful and voluptuous, the young woman who stood before her now looked haggard, tired and ten years older than Shelby.

"I tried to find you a couple of times after I got home from law school, but no luck. I've missed you."

"You're so sweet, Shelby. You always were. I don't know how I would've gotten through high school without your friendship."

"Well, that works both ways. How in the world would I ever have learned how to curl my eyelashes without yanking them all out if it hadn't been for you?"

Yvette smiled warmly. "We had some good times, didn't we?"

"And some great slumber parties." Shelby gave Yvette's shoulder a squeeze. "I'm really glad to see you. Are you still living in New Orleans?"

"I did for a while, then I sorta…moved around. I moved back here about a month ago."

"A month! And you're just now getting in touch with me. Shame on you, Yvette." Out of habit, Shelby reached into her purse for her business card, then stopped. "What am I doing? You know my phone number. Lord knows, we spent enough hours on the phone when we were teenagers." She handed her the card anyway. "This will save you looking up the office number. I want you to call me so we can go to lunch tomorrow, okay?"

When Yvette didn't make a move to take the card, Shelby asked, "Are you all right? You look a little pale. Why don't you come inside where it's cool?"

"No." Again, she glanced nervously down the street. "I, uh, hear you're a real lawyer now. Passed the bar and everything, huh?"

"Yes."

"I'm real happy for you. It's what you always wanted."

"Yvette, something *is* wrong. I insist you come inside and—"

Suddenly Yvette began to sob. "Oh, Shelby," she cried. "You've got to help me. You've just got to."

Shelby slipped her arm around Yvette's shoulders again. "Of course I will. Now, just try to calm yourself and tell me what's wrong."

"I'm so desperate. You're the only one…the only one I can turn to."

"Take a deep breath and tell me what this is all about."

"My baby," Yvette sobbed. "He's gonna take my baby. Oh, God. Please, please, Shelby, you've just got to help me."

# CHAPTER FIVE

YVETTE AVENALL WAS a physical and emotional wreck, and Shelby practically had to carry her across the parking lot and into the building. Once inside, she insisted her friend lie down on the sofa in her office while she got her a glass of water and some tissues. But it was several minutes before Yvette could pull herself together enough to talk without sobbing.

"Now…" Shelby smoothed a strand of naturally flaxen hair away from her friend's heart-shaped face. "You want to tell me what this is all about? Who is *he?* And why is he trying to take your child?"

"He's the father, but he's no good, Shelby. He doesn't love Dante. He's—"

"Easy. I assume Dante is your baby. What's the father's name?"

Yvette stopped crying, and a look of sheer terror crossed her face. "Lyle Masson," she whispered.

Shelby's mouth fell open, but she had the good grace to recover quickly. Yvette had just named one of Louisiana's most influential businessmen as her child's father. Masson was wealthy, powerful…and married.

"I know what you're thinking," Yvette said at the shocked expression on Shelby's face. "But it isn't what you think. I mean it is, but it wasn't in the beginning."

"Why don't you start at the beginning and explain."

"But you'll be my lawyer, won't you? I can't pay a...what do you call those things..."

"Retainer?"

"Yeah, that's it. They said I better not cause any trouble."

"Who told you that?"

"Two men. They knocked on my door this morning, and they weren't very nice."

"Slow down. Let's take this one step at a time."

"Everything I tell you will be confidential, right? I mean, since you're my lawyer, you—"

"Yvette, I'm not sure you need me advising you. Family law is extremely complicated, and I'm inexperienced. However, we do have a highly qualified attorney with the firm—"

"No. I..." Yvette shoved her fingers through her hair, but the thick blond strands fell back against her face. "H-how much will this guy charge?"

Truthfully, the answer was a lot. Alan Renquist was one of the best, and his fee reflected his success. "Well..."

"I don't have a lot of money. I was hoping you might, uh—" she glanced away, clearly embarrassed "—let me pay it out." Then her gaze slid back and locked with Shelby's. "I'll sign a note. I'll do whatever you ask, and I promise to pay you if it takes the rest of my life. But there's no one else. Nowhere I can go...please, Shelby," she begged.

One of the reasons she and Yvette had become such close friends the summer before their senior year in high school was they had both lost their mothers that year—Yvette's to cancer, Shelby's to...well, whatever reason her mother had considered justifiable for leaving. Yvette's father had never been around, either, and she had no brothers or sisters—as far as Shelby knew, no other family in Bayou Beltane.

"I mean it about the money. No matter what it takes, I'll pay you."

"Don't give money another thought," Shelby assured her. "I'm taking your case on a fee-waived basis. Pro bono, if you will."

"Oh, no, I can't let you—"

Shelby stopped her. "Yvette, you were there for me when no one else understood how hurt I was. When not even my own family could comfort me. I've shared my deepest secrets with you, and vice versa. We're friends, and friends help each other. Now—" she smiled "—no more talk about paying me."

Yvette closed her eyes and sighed. "Thank you, Shelby." When she opened them again they were bright with hope.

"You'll need to sign a fee-waived agreement, but as of now, I'm your attorney. Anything you say to me is privileged, confidential. By law, I can't repeat a word without your permission. So tell me the problem."

Yvette dug into the fold of her hobo bag, withdrew an envelope and handed it to her friend. "The two men gave this to me."

Shelby opened it and glanced over the document. "This is a petition for determination of paternity and a petition for custody."

"Does that mean Lyle is going to get Dante?"

"Not necessarily. It just means that his lawyer has asked the court to determine if he's Dante's father, and if so, to grant full custody. That doesn't mean he'll win.''

"You won't let him, will you, Shelby? Dante is my whole life. I don't know what I'd do if I lost him.''

"First things first. You're positive that Lyle Masson is your baby's father?''

"Yes, but Dante's not a baby. He's five years old.''

"According to this petition, Masson only recently learned of the boy's existence.''

"That's a lie. He's known from the day I found out I was pregnant.''

"Okay, tell me how you got to this point.''

"How far back do you want me to go?''

"Start when you met Masson.''

"Well, after high school I moved to New Orleans. There were these girls living in my apartment building. They all worked for this modeling agency.''

"Modeling agency?'' Shelby asked, still scanning the reasons listed on the custody request.

"Yeah. They helped me get a job there. Oh, I don't mean as a model. Mercy, I'm not pretty enough for anything like that, but the agency needed a receptionist and they put in a good word for me. Anyway, after I'd been working there about a month they invited me to a party. That's where I met Lyle, and we started dating.''

"Didn't you know he was married?''

"Not at first. I didn't even know who he was, or what he did. You know me, Shelby. I never paid much attention to the society page or who's who.''

"When did you find out he was married?''

She ducked her head. "After we had been going out steady for over two months. By time I was crazy in love with him.'' Yvette looked up. ''He offered to set me up in my own apartment.''

''I see,'' Shelby said, trying hard to remain professional and nonjudgmental. ''Then what happened?''

''We...dated for almost a year, then I got pregnant. I didn't mean to. But I was so in love with Lyle I never thought he would react the way he did.''

''I take it Masson wasn't pleased.''

''He went nuts. Started screaming at me to get rid of it. I told him that was a mortal sin, and I couldn't do it. He really went crazy then, accusing me of setting him up all along so I could blackmail him with a bastard kid. He was—'' a fresh tear spilled down Yvette's cheek ''—so mean.''

Shelby took Yvette's trembling hand in hers. ''Did he hit you?''

The tears flowed unchecked as she whispered, ''Yes.''

''Bad?''

A single nod was the response.

Shelby waited, knowing her friend needed a moment to herself before she continued. ''Then what happened?'' she asked finally.

''He told me to get out. That he didn't ever wanna see me or my brat again. And if I ever came around looking for money, he'd sic the dogs on me. Those girls I mentioned—'' she sniffed and dabbed at her eyes ''—got me to a doctor and put me up for the night. But before sunup the next day I went back to the apartment, got my things, left the key and never looked back. I went to one of the Sisters of Charity homes until Dante was born. They helped me get a job working in a bookstore. Dante and I had a small apartment over the store, and I worked up to manager.

We had to pinch pennies, but it wasn't too bad. I should have known that sooner or later Lyle would come looking for Dante, especially after the accident.''

"Accident?"

"Last year his wife and nine-year-old daughter were in a car wreck. The little girl died.''

"Yes," Shelby said. "I vaguely remember reading about it.''

"Well, his wife can't have any more babies. So now he wants his son.''

"Why now? Why did he wait a year?''

"Because he's gonna go into politics. I bet he told me a thousand times how he had it all planned out. He's on those school boards and committees and stuff, and he gives a ton of money to his political party. He's just been bidin' his time. When the state elections come up in two years, he's gonna run. That was always his plan.''

"Then, why would he want Dante? If he's the father, he'll be publicly admitting to an extramarital affair. I would think his wife might object. Strongly.''

"No. She does whatever Lyle tells her to. Anyway, two years from now everybody will have forgotten.''

Shelby was beginning to get a clear picture of Lyle Masson's motives—a very clear but ugly picture. *Greed can make the most handsome person unattractive,* she thought, remembering her own experience with an ambitious man. "And by coming forth to admit paternity and offering Dante a home with all the advantages money can buy, Masson looks like an honest man. Very clever.''

"Oh, he's real smart all right. Don't underestimate

him, Shelby. He usually gets what he wants no matter who it hurts.''

"Obviously. Yvette, have you read this petition?''

She shook her head. ''I just saw what it was, and saw Lyle's name, and I panicked. You were the first person I thought of to come to for help.''

"I won't bore you with all the legal language, but essentially, Lyle is accusing you of being an unfit mother due to your former career as a prostitute.''

Yvette shot off the sofa. ''That's not true, and he knows it.''

"But the modeling agency *was* a front for a call-girl operation, wasn't it?''

"I—I didn't know it at first, but…yeah.''

"But you never actually participated?'' When she didn't answer, Shelby grew uncomfortable. ''Yvette, I need to know everything. The whole truth.''

"The second night I met Lyle was the first time I ever, you know…for money.''

"He paid you for sex?''

Yvette winced, but to her credit didn't try to duck the question. ''Yes,'' she said.

"And after that night?''

"No. Lyle called the next day and invited me out, and the next. Then he offered to move me into a nicer apartment, but he wanted me to quit the modeling agency, so I did.''

"And this is the first time Masson has attempted to contact you in over five years?''

"Yes. I saw him once down on Canal Street during Mardi Gras, but he didn't see me. At least I don't think he did.''

Shelby thought for a moment. ''I wonder how he found out where you live? Any ideas?''

"No."

"Well, I think the first order of business is to contact Masson's lawyer." Then Shelby remembered something Yvette had said a few moments earlier. "What did you mean when you said the two men told you not to cause any trouble?"

"They said if I kicked up a fuss over this, I'd be sorry. They said if I was smart, I'd give Dante to Lyle and wind up a wealthy woman. If I didn't, I'd wind up with nothing."

Shelby leaned back in her chair. "Why didn't you run? It worked once before."

"You don't know Lyle. Now that he's found me, I couldn't run far enough or fast enough. He has a lot of power, Shelby. And he knows a lot of powerful people, including your uncle Philip."

"What does my uncle Philip have to do with this?"

"Nothing really, except he used to come to the Men's Club meetings at my apartment."

"Men's Club?"

"That's what Lyle called it. Usually five or six men. I couldn't tell you names, because I was never introduced, but I've seen some of their pictures in the paper."

"What went on at these meetings?"

Yvette shrugged. "Lyle always made me leave. I'd go shopping for a few hours, or to a movie. But I had to call and make sure the meeting was over before I could come home."

What Yvette described might be nothing more than a businessman entertaining politicians, but the fact that Philip Delacroix was involved automatically made Shelby suspicious. She had never understood how two men could be as totally different as her grandfather and his brother. Where Charles had worked hard to build a solid, reputable firm, beyond reproach in every way, Philip had aligned himself with power brokers and ruthless men whose reputations were often suspect.

"What does the Men's Club have to do with Lyle taking Dante?"

"I don't know. Maybe nothing," Yvette replied. She reached for another tissue.

The more Shelby thought about it, the more she realized this case might turn out to be much more than merely a custody battle. With the petition in her hand, she walked over to her desk and began making some notes. "It could take me a couple of days to set up an appointment with Masson's attorney. Meanwhile, I'll go over everything you've told me with Alan and—"

Yvette jumped up from the sofa. "But you can't. You said you wouldn't!"

"When you hired me as your attorney, you hired this firm. Whatever I tell Alan is still privileged. That goes for the research assistants who work on your case, and the secretary who inputs your data into the computer."

"Oh." Yvette sat back down.

"Now, I need you to stay calm and try not to worry. I'll call today and attempt to set up an appointment with Masson's lawyer, and we'll go from there. In the meantime, I need your home phone and office number. Oh, and I'll need you to gather all Dante's medical records and his birth certificate. Also I think it would be a good idea if we had some character witnesses that might be willing to give a deposition. Can you get in touch with the retired bookstore owner?''

''No.''

''Why not?''

''He died.''

''What about your current employer?''

''The Book Nook.''

''The one that just opened up down by the old depot? Are you the manager?''

''The owner.''

Shelby was surprised. ''I don't understand. You just told me you were broke.''

''As broke as broke can be. Every dime I had went into moving back here and setting up the bookstore.''

''And, knowing how this town isn't exactly inclined to welcome newcomers with open arms, I'm sure it's a struggle.''

''I figured since I grew up here it might make a difference, but it's slow. Real slow.''

''Are you okay? I mean, you and Dante aren't—''

Yvette squared her shoulders. ''We're hangin' on.''

''Good,'' Shelby said, making a mental note to drop by the store and order books rather than drive to Slidell or into New Orleans. ''Well, I think that will get the ball rolling.''

Yvette came over to her. ''I'll never be able to thank you enough, Shelby. Not in a million years.''

''I haven't done anything yet.''

''Oh, yes you have. You've given me the courage to deal with this. Before, I didn't know where to turn, what to do. Now I've got someone on my side.''

''I promise I'll do my best for you, Yvette. I won't leave a stone unturned to get to the truth and help you keep your son. I may not be all that experienced, but I'm tenacious as hell.''

Yvette smiled, and though Shelby hated to interject reality, she had to add, "This may be a simple, straightforward custody battle that, hopefully, can be settled out of court. Then again, it may not. And you need to think about the possibility that you may have to give Masson visitation rights in order to retain custody.''

"I don't want Dante anywhere near Connie Masson.''

"That's understandable. And I'm not saying that's what you'll have to do, but I want to prepare you for some contingencies. The firm Masson has hired is top-notch. We've got our work cut out for us.''

"But you...you do think you can win?"

Shelby smiled and gave her friend a pat on the shoulder. "That's the goal, and I'm going to give it everything I've got.''

"Thank goodness you haven't changed. What happens next?''

"Next we deny everything.''

"But Lyle is—''

"Yvette, we have fifteen days to respond to this petition, and using general denial will buy us some time. Eventually, you and Dante will have to submit to blood testing to see if there is a DNA match.''

"But I thought the paper meant Lyle admitted to being Dante's father.''

"The court still has to have proof. Now, it'll take four to six weeks to get the results, and by that time, hopefully we can find a witness to verify that Masson knew about the baby and that he abandoned you when you refused to have an abortion.''

"But what if we can't do that?"

"First things first. I'll talk to Masson's attorney. For now, go home, kiss your son, and I'll call you," she told her as they walked back outside.

As she watched Yvette get into her car and drive away, Shelby hoped she hadn't bitten off more than she could chew.

TRAVIS CANCELED his appointment to see the other mare and instead called the private detective he'd hired, a Mr. Dale Foster. He had to leave two messages before Foster returned his call.

"I've got very little so far, Mr. Hardin. Some old newspaper clippings, couple of articles in a society magazine published in the late thirties, which folded after the war started. I do expect to have what you wanted on Charles Delacroix by tomorrow noon."

"Check out Philip Delacroix while you're at it, okay?"

"Charles's twin brother. Okay, I'll see what I can come up with. Anyone else?"

Travis thought about Shelby for a moment, then decided against it. "No."

"I'll be in touch," Foster said, and hung up.

# CHAPTER SIX

TRAVIS DECIDED TO CANCEL his date with Shelby no less than three times. And each time he changed his mind. He was going through with this if it killed him. Part of his hesitation stemmed from the fact that he didn't feel comfortable walking into Charles Delacroix's house. Travis would much rather have met her at the park again. Another part stemmed from the fact that the thought of spending an entire evening fighting his attraction to Shelby didn't sound like a fun time. But he *was* attracted to her, and it wasn't decreasing, much less disappearing.

Listening to her talk about family loyalty hadn't bolstered his hope that she might not want to kill him outright when she found out who he was and what he was up to. Travis hated being deliberately deceitful, but there was no other way. And what Shelby didn't know wouldn't hurt her. At least, that was the justification running through his mind as he pulled up before her home just as dusk cast its shadows.

So this was Riverwood, he thought, gazing at the two-story house with its gallery, six Doric columns and precisely tended, rolling lawn. It was so typical of the picture-postcard image of a Southern plantation-style home that he half expected to hear the theme from *Gone With the Wind* drifting through the windows. The place was more spacious-looking than sprawling, more stately than grand, but undeniably impressive.

Exactly what he had expected from the Delacroix. Riverwood made an unmistakable statement—namely that money, power and tradition were what counted.

He got out of his truck and stood for a moment just looking at the house. Then he climbed the wide steps up to the porch and rang the bell.

Shelby answered the door. "Hi."

"Hanging pictures, or should I duck?" he asked, pointing to the shoe in her hand.

"Oh, no. C'mon in."

When he stepped inside, she reached out to him, and for a split second he thought she intended to put her arms around his neck. Instead, she put her hand on his shoulder for balance and slipped off her other shoe. The move surprised him, but even more surprising was his disappointment that she hadn't embraced him.

"I just walked in the door a few moments ago, and I couldn't stand these shoes another second. In fact—" she tossed both shoes onto a chair on the other side of the door "—I'm seriously considering giving them to my brother's dog as punishment for the way they've abused my toes."

"Sic the dogs on 'em, huh?"

Shelby laughed. "Something like that. I apologize for not being ready, but it's been one of those days. In fact..." She looked up at him and suddenly realized they were practically in an embrace.

Travis looked into her face and saw not only fatigue, but worry. The urge to touch her cheek, to reassure her, was so powerful it almost took his breath away. *Don't go there,* he warned himself. He needed distance, yet he made no effort to move away from her. "In fact?" he asked when she didn't continue.

"What?"

"You were saying?"

"Uh, I don't remember." She shook her head as if to clear it. "Sorry, my brain must be as tired as my feet. If you don't mind waiting for a few more minutes, I'll run upstairs and change." She turned to go, but his hand on her arm stopped her.

"Darlin', if you'd rather do Commander's Palace another time, it's all right by me. Gotta admit, I'm not much on fancy, anyway."

Travis couldn't believe he was letting her off so easy. But here he was, giving her an out. And realizing he would be disappointed if she didn't take it.

"Are you saying you want to call the evening off?"

"Hold your horses. I just figured you're beat, and it's a long drive. I'm offering a rain check on the dinner, but I sure hope you're not ready to run me off."

Shelby covered his hand with hers. "You are the sweetest man, Travis Hardin. And I'm most certainly not ready to run you off. How in the world have the women in Texas let you slip through their fingers?"

"Being smart, probably. I'm no prize, darlin'." Unless you considered him a prize heel.

*Darlin'.* She liked the sound of that. "Maybe they just don't know a diamond in the rough when they see one." She raised herself on tiptoe and kissed his cheek. "I have it on good authority that there's a bottle of Chablis sitting right next to a plate of cold fried chicken in our refrigerator, and at least two slices of chocolate cake left. Interested?"

"You got a deal, but—" he glanced around "—won't that upset dinner for everybody else?"

"Granddad is having dinner with Aunt Mary and Uncle William. Jax is still at the stables, and probably will be until well after dark. Beau, that's my brother, is in New Orleans for some charity thing. He's staying there overnight."

"What about your father?"

"He's in Baton Rouge and not due back for several days." Shelby smiled. "There's just you, me and the chicken."

"Sounds mighty cozy."

Her smile widened. "I'm going to dash upstairs, change, and I'll be back. Five minutes, tops." And she was gone.

Travis took off his jacket and draped it over a nearby chair. He had a second chance to see if Shelby knew anything about her granddaddy's past, and he told himself not to blow it. All he had to do was remember to keep his mind on business. Not a cinch to do with Shelby in the vicinity. Despite the fact that he was attracted to her, he was discovering that he liked her. He liked her wit and her zest for life.

"I'm back."

He turned to find her dressed in jeans and a sexy little sweater that stopped barely past her navel. Lord, but she looked good in those jeans. Even better than yesterday. "I, uh, took off my coat. Hope you don't mind."

"Of course not. Make yourself comfortable." Not only had he ditched the jacket, but he had rolled up his sleeves, as well. Was it her imagination or did he get better-looking every time she saw him? "C'mon," she said, leading the way to the kitchen.

Travis discovered he had been wrong when he hadn't considered Riverwood sprawling. The farther he went into the house, the bigger it seemed to get. Judging from the size of the first floor, which contained the small parlor where he had waited, a dining room, another larger parlor with a baby grand piano, a kitchen and at least one bathroom, he estimated there must be five or six bedrooms upstairs. When they reached the kitchen, he noticed a breezeway that connected to what looked like a small guest house. Several hundred yards behind the guest house was a cottage. The lights were on, and he wondered if that was the servants' quarters.

Shelby opened the refrigerator, removed the wine, the chicken and a bowl of fruit. "Oh, boy, are you in luck. Not only leftover chicken, but some of Odelle's deviled eggs, as well."

"Odelle?"

"Odelle Raison. She and her husband, Woodrow, look after all of us. Odelle is housekeeper and cook, and Woodrow takes care of the lawn and cars. If you met my grandfather yesterday, Woodrow was his driver. They've been here for as long as I can remember, and they're part of our family."

"All of us?"

"Grandfather, my dad, my sister Jax, whom you've already met, and my brother, Beau."

"Sounds like our bunkhouse."

Shelby laughed. "Not a bad analogy, but those of us still at Riverwood are so busy and lead such separate lives, it's seldom we're all in the house at the same time. Actually, Jax lives in a cottage that Grandfather renovated about fifteen years ago. But she's not exactly the domestic type, so she takes most of her meals with us.''

''You said 'Those of us still at Riverwood.' Don't tell me there're more Delacroix?''

''Just my sister Charly, who just graduated from the New Orleans Police Acadamy, and my sister Marie, who lives in New Orleans. We Delacroix are a prolific bunch.''

''So, you've lived here all your life?''

''Literally, except for when I was at college,'' she told him while she dished fruit into two small bowls. ''In fact—would you hand me a couple of napkins out of the drawer behind you?''

Travis found the napkins and handed them to her.

''I was born right upstairs, second bedroom on the left.'' She put two pieces of chicken on Travis's plate and one on hers, then added the same ratio of deviled eggs. Then she thought about the size of the meal he had consumed at the Catfish Shack, and added another piece of chicken. ''I showed up a couple of weeks early and in a hurry. Threw the whole house into a tailspin.''

Travis grinned. ''Now, why doesn't that surprise me?'' He wished she would stop reaching for things. Every time she moved, so did the little sweater, giving him a glimpse of her belly button. Not that he had a thing for belly buttons, but just the way the hem of the sweater played peek-a-boo was driving him crazy.

''But as I said before, tonight it's just you, me and the chicken.'' As soon as the words were out of her mouth, Shelby realized this was the first time she had been truly alone with a man in three years. Again, there were no nerves. She was completely at ease with Travis.

"There." She put her hands on her hips and surveyed her handiwork. "That's about as creative as I get in the kitchen. Let's see—" she turned around and yanked open a drawer "—I know there's a corkscrew in here…" She turned back to him, holding her prize. "Ta-da! Will you do the honors?"

Travis opened the wine, retrieved two glasses per Shelby's directions, and together they carried their meal through the kitchen to what had probably been a screened-in porch at one time, but was now an enclosed solarium and garden room with more windows than walls. They sat down at a small, glass-topped white wicker table with two chairs.

"Find a mare?"

"Not yet."

She took a sip of wine. "Oh, I almost forgot. Did you find out anything about your relatives?"

She had given him the perfect opening, and he knew he should take it. "Naw," he said after a moment. "Now, you, on the other hand, could probably make one phone call to research your ancestors back six generations."

"No doubt there's tons of records."

"Your ancestry's full of lawyers, I'll bet."

She took a bite of deviled egg, then dabbed at her mouth with the corner of her napkin. "No. My great-grandfather Hamilton started the firm right after the First World War. He was something of a legend in Louisiana law. My grandfather and great-uncle Philip are both lawyers, as are my father and two cousins, Joanna and Drew. The rest of the Delacroix offspring have fallen by the legal wayside, so to speak."

Travis stabbed a piece of chicken with his fork. "All except you."

"My father says my first word was actually a question—'What?' I've been asking questions ever since. Still, there are days…" Shelby rubbed the back of her neck. "Days like today, I wonder why I bothered."

"Bad day?"

"Frustrating," she said. "I hate seeing people with power trying to control someone else's life."

"Those underdogs again?"

"I suppose. What it really boils down to is that I hate injustice. It doesn't make any difference who, what or where, I can't tolerate it. No one is above the law, no matter how much money or power they possess. And I know what you're thinking," she added as she picked up both plates and headed back to the kitchen. Travis followed her. "The law is manipulated every day. We see it regularly on the evening news, but that doesn't mean we should just throw up our hands and say, 'Oh, well.'"

The fire in her eyes told him she wasn't spouting platitudes or looking for a soapbox. This was a statement of her values and beliefs, a definition of Shelby. Even while Travis cautioned himself not to hope her zeal might extend to him when she discovered his identity, he did. "You've got a real fire for this, don't you, darlin'?"

"Yes, I do. Everyone, and I mean everyone, should be treated equally under the law. Guess that makes me sound like an idiotic idealist, doesn't it?"

"Not in my book. Darlin', there's no sin in being passionate about your work, or your family."

"That's not always a positive. I have a tendency

to act too quickly sometimes. Leap before I look, so to speak. Like when I kissed you last night.''

The unexpected statement caught him off guard, but he recovered with a little humor. ''Wanna take it back?''

Shelby grinned. ''No. But I didn't think about how you might react, and I should have. I certainly know better. I mean, for most men, that's all the green light they need. You could have pressed your advantage. Why didn't you?''

What could he say? *I probably wouldn't have kissed you if I had known who you were.* Frankly, he wasn't sure just how honest that statement would be. ''Not my style, darlin','' he said nonchalantly.

''What is your style?''

''Slow and easy.''

Oh, my, Shelby thought. How could three words sound so incredibly sensual? The thought of Travis making slow, easy love to her set her nerves tingling. ''That's exactly what I'm talking about.''

''What?''

''You say 'slow and easy,' and I automatically start thinking about what comes next.''

He was on the verge of asking her what she wanted to come next, but decided he wasn't prepared for her answer.

Shelby peered at him. ''Uh-oh. Are you starting to panic?''

''Do I look like a man who panics easily?''

''No, but if you are, I can put your mind at rest. I told you I like you, Travis. More than I've liked anyone in a long time. But I'm not hearing wedding bells when I kiss you, if that's what you're worried about.''

''Do I look worried?'' The fact of the matter was,

he liked her, too. More than he should. And he *was* worried. She was so direct, so honest that he had a hard time thinking of her as part of the "evil Delacroix." Dangerous thinking.

"No." She smiled, moving closer to him. "At the moment you look well fed and very handsome."

And she looked beautiful. Beautiful and tempting. Before now, Travis hadn't fully understood how difficult it would be to maintain his distance while trying to get information from her. The more he was with her, the stronger the attraction became. He had to lighten the mood, back off.

"You wouldn't be trying to turn my head with your lawyer sweet talk, now, would you, darlin'?"

"Just stating the facts."

"Speaking of stating facts, didn't you mention something about chocolate cake?"

"Cake and coffee coming up," she said. "Why don't you go on to the parlor, and I'll bring it in."

Travis was glad to put some distance between them. He had to do better than this or he would be in deep trouble where Shelby was concerned. He was on his way back to the small parlor when the piano caught his eye. What he knew about musical instruments could be inscribed on the head of a straight pin, but it didn't take an expert to recognize the name Steinway. The piano dominated the parlor—he supposed they referred to it as the music room—and its smooth ebony surface gleamed like a mirror.

"There you are," Shelby said, carrying a tray with the cake and coffee.

Travis took the tray and set it on a table in front of the Victorian settee directly across from the piano. "Do you play?"

"No. My grandfather used to play. So did my dad. I had a few lessons, but I'm afraid I've got a tin ear. My sister Marie plays beautifully."

"This house is outstanding," he said, hoping to steer the conversation away from anything personal. "How old is it?"

"Turn of the century, I think. Or shortly before. Granddad had it modernized, I guess you would say, in the 1930s. Electricity, new plumbing, additional bathrooms, that sort of thing. He also added the guest house and servants' quarters, and renovated the cottage Jax lives in."

It was beginning to sound like a lot more than just his great-aunt's murder had happened in 1938, and Travis was betting all of it was connected somehow. "Thought you said your great-granddaddy started the law firm after World War I."

"He did. Granddad grew up at Belle Terre. It's what you might call the old family plantation. My great-uncle Philip still lives there with his son, Drew. His daughter Joanna lived there for a while after her husband died, but not anymore. She also used to work for her father, but that's over, too. Just recently she walked away from Uncle Philip's firm and came to work with us."

When Travis raised an eyebrow, Shelby added, "I told you he was a real piece of work. I wouldn't call him a crook, at least not to his face, but let's just say he uses the law."

"Quite a collection of folks. They're…"

"Eccentric? Colorful? All of the above?"

"Yeah."

"We do have our moments. But then, I think that's probably true of most families. What about yours?"

Travis shook his head. "Can't compete. I come from plain old hard-working cowboys and riggers."

"Riggers?"

"Oil-field workers. My great-grandparents had a run of bad luck, lost everything, and they were, uh, forced to relocate to Texas. The only steady work was in the East Texas oil fields."

"So how did you get from rigs to ranches?"

"The hard way." She was asking *him* questions instead of the other way around. Travis glanced around the room, his mind searching for another topic of conversation. Then he spotted a Victrola in the corner and moved toward it. "Hey, does that thing work?"

"I think so." He never seems to want to talk about himself, Shelby thought, picking up a plate of the chocolate cake. Maybe he was just a private person. "Ready for your cake?"

"Hmm, not just yet," Travis said, giving his attention to examining the old phonograph.

While she ate her cake, Travis cranked up the machine, moved the needle into place, and the scratchy strains of a song filled the room. "Casey would waltz with a strawberry blonde, and the band played on…"

"Too bad I'm a brunette."

Travis grinned. "You don't get off that easy, darlin'. I've got two left feet, and they've both been stepped on by too many horses, but may I have the honor of a dance?" Tugging her to her feet, he swept her into his arms and around the floor.

It was a silly, frivolous thing to do, twirling to an old tune in the middle of the music room. And Shelby loved it. Strange, but in the short time since meeting Travis, she had become acutely aware that there were a great many things she had been missing. Things like unplanned, unqualified fun. And this delicious feeling of freedom and spontaneity was certainly near the top of the list.

"You do not have two left feet," she told him as they danced past the piano and into the wide foyer. "You're very smooth."

"Must be my partner."

Instinctively, he pulled her closer as they swayed to the music, their bodies gently moving against each other. She was so warm, so soft in his arms, and it was so easy to pretend they were just a man and a woman enjoying each other. No past, just the present. When she smiled up at him, it was all he could do to keep from kissing her. But kissing her was not in his plan, Travis reminded himself, gazing into her soft eyes. Kissing her would be a mistake. But need was tough competition for reason, and before he realized his intention, his mouth claimed hers. Reason never stood a chance.

She tasted of chocolate and temptation, and the combination went straight to Travis's head. He slid his hands up her back, pulling her to him.

While he put up a valiant struggle, with what remained of his willpower, it was a lost cause. He wanted to possess and devour her—unleash her desire and at the same time lose himself in it. He had never responded to a woman this way, and part of him resented her for that. But he couldn't hang on to his resentment. One touch of her mouth to his, and he forgot what had driven him from Texas to Louisiana. She *was* the fantasy he had seen from the first. All silk and satin, melting against him, yet at the same time sweet and soft.

When Shelby wrapped her arms around his neck, murmuring in pleasure, the sound went through Travis like a rifle shot, yanking him back to reality. He was a heartbeat away from making a fool out of himself, he realized, finally drawing away. He stared at her, her lips swollen from his bruising kiss, and knew she had no idea how close she had come to being ravished.

Travis forced himself to breathe deeply for several seconds before he decided he was capable of coherent speech. *Easy does it,* he reminded himself.

"It's…getting late," he said, trying to keep his tone calm. "And I think it's time for me to go."

"So soon?"

He tried to smile, tried to lighten the mood, but knew it was a poor job at best. "Darlin', it's either leave after dinner or stay for breakfast." She would never know how true his words were.

"Oh." She blushed.

If Travis needed anything to validate the good sense he had just exhibited, her blush did the trick. She was just too sweet for her own good, he thought. And while he was using her to help him get information, he couldn't, wouldn't use her emotions, as well. Not even his grandmother's dying request could justify that.

"Thanks for the supper. Home cookin' beats cafés any day."

"You're welcome."

"I'll call you." He turned and headed for the front door.

"Travis?"

When he stopped and turned toward her, she

walked to him, rose up on her toes and kissed his cheek. "Thank you."

Without another word, he left.

As she watched him drive away, Shelby sighed, wondering if knights ever wore cowboy boots.

THE PHONE WAS RINGING when Travis walked into his motel room, and he grabbed it. "Travis Hardin."

"Hey, boy."

"Dad! How are you?"

"Fine. Where you been? I been callin' for the last hour."

"Having supper with Shelby Delacroix."

"And?"

"Philip Delacroix seems to be the shady character in the family, but still nothing on Charles. I expect something from Foster tomorrow. And I'm driving to Covington in the morning to check out the newspaper files. Maybe something will turn up."

"You sound tired, son," T.C. said.

"More like frustrated. I don't think I'm cut out for this double-life kinda stuff."

"And I'm right sorry you got to go through it. But you'll do fine."

"Yeah."

"Gimme a call tomorrow when you hear from Foster."

"Sure. 'Night, Dad."

For as long as Travis could remember he had shared his problems with his dad, and together they had found a solution. They had a solid understanding, but Travis didn't think T.C. would understand his feelings about Shelby. Hell, he wasn't sure he understood them himself. All he knew was that in a short time she had become very important to him. A week ago he would have said it was impossible to feel anything but lust after knowing a woman for only two days. But that was before he'd met Shelby.

She was on his mind constantly. In any other situation, she was exactly the kind of woman he could be serious about. The kind of woman he could take home to meet his dad. But, of course, the situation was what it was.

And getting serious about Shelby just wasn't in his plans.

# CHAPTER SEVEN

DAYDREAMING ABOUT TRAVIS, Shelby walked into her office fifteen minutes late the following morning, and found no less than three messages from Yvette Avenall. All marked urgent.

There was also a message from Lyle Masson's attorney.

Shelby dialed Yvette's number and got an answer on the first ring. "Book Nook."

"Yvette, this is Shelby. I'm sor—"

"Shelby! Thank goodness you've called. Those men were here again."

"The ones you told me about yesterday?"

"Yeah."

"They didn't threaten you, did they?"

"No. They offered me money."

"Yvette, you didn't take it, did you?"

"No."

"Or let those men into your apartment?"

"Good Lord, no! I talked through the door and looked through the peephole. Then I told them to go away and not come back."

"Good. If they show up again, tell them you can't talk to anyone about this matter without your attorney present."

"You think they'll come back?"

"Very likely. How much money did they offer you?"

"Fifty thousand dollars."

Shelby wasn't really surprised, but the sum was more substantial than she'd expected. Lyle Masson had deep pockets and heavyweight connections. He'd probably like nothing better than for Yvette to take the money and conveniently disappear.

"Did you see the money, or a check?" A check would be too good to be true, since it could be traced, but Shelby could hope.

"They held up a stack of bills, but I couldn't see real good. No tellin' how much was there. It could have been fifty thousand."

"Can you describe the men to me?"

"One was tall, built like a wrestler, and he was bald. You know, like he shaved his whole head. The other one was not so big, and he had hair. Long, dark hair, and he wore those mirrored sunglasses. Both times. And this morning was cloudy. Shelby, can you fix it so they don't come around anymore? They scare me."

"I'll see what I can do."

Privately, Shelby thought Yvette might have good reason to be frightened, considering the men she had just described were probably Masson's bodyguards. He had some very powerful friends, and not all of them were accepted in polite society. He had also been rumored to be involved in several minor political scandals over the last few years, but never anything substantial.

"I have a message to call Lyle's attorney, and I'm sure it's to set up a meeting now that he knows you have legal counsel. Let me call you back as soon as I've spoken to him.''

''Okay.''

Shelby hung up and immediately dialed the number of Masson's law firm. She was not only surprised to learn Walter Trowbridge was Masson's attorney, but also that he would be in Covington that day and wanted to stop by Delacroix and Associates for a meeting. The time was set for midafternoon.

This was all way too convenient, Shelby thought. Too easy. Trowbridge was a high-priced divorce attorney and had a reputation for being ruthless in custody battles. His forte was representing his wealthy male friends when they got ready to move on to the next wife. Shelby decided he must have a trick or two up his sleeve to be so accommodating. So be it. She had approximately five hours to prepare for this meeting and she needed help. She dialed Alan Renquist's office, and fortunately he had some time for her. Renquist knew Trowbrige well, and Shelby was counting on picking his brain.


''MR. HARDIN.''

''Yeah, Foster? Find anything?''

''Do you have access to a fax machine?''

''There's one in the motel office,'' Travis said, and gave him the number.

''So far I've turned up newspaper clippings from New Orleans, Covington, Bayou Beltane and even Baton Rouge. This was big news in '38.''

''What about the background check on Charles?''

''He's clean as a whistle. So far.''

''He can't be.''

''I've gone deep, Mr. Hardin. His firm is highly

respected. He's got a solid reputation in the legal community. Honest, civic-minded and known to take pro bono cases most other firms wouldn't touch. Everybody connected to his firm gives him high marks from when he ran the place. As far as the murder goes, he was a witness for the prosecution, and, well…''

''Well what?''

''According to the articles, he testified in open court to being in love with your great-aunt.''

Travis had a hard time imagining the distant, formal man he had met talking about love in public. But then, no one stayed the same for sixty years. ''Look, Foster, this is all fine, but I want to know what he was like in college. I want to know if he cheated on exams, drank too much, ran with a wild crowd. The man might be benevolent gentry now, but chances are he didn't start out that way. Dig deeper.''

''All right.''

''What about Philip?''

''Mr. Hardin, the motel office probably doesn't have enough paper for me to fax what I've got on the twin brother.''

''Then, send a hard copy overnight.''

''You got it,'' Foster said, and hung up.

Travis left his room and went to the office. He couldn't believe the report on Charles had turned out almost pristine. There had to be more. Maybe the newspaper articles would reveal something Foster had missed. A short fifteen minutes later he had the faxes spread out on the table in his motel room.

The account of the arrest and trial of Rafael Perdido had made front-page news for almost two weeks. During that time, the newspaper reporter had made only a halfhearted attempt not to prejudice his readers against Perdido. It was clear that even back in 1938 the media had the power to sway opinions.

According to the articles, twenty-two-year-old Perdido had wandered into Bayou Beltane and had worked at odd jobs for a couple of months before the murder. He'd spent a lot of his money and spare time at a pool hall in a seedy section of town, and was known to be a "hard drinker." He had also demonstrated a quick and nasty temper on more than one occasion, and had been arrested in New Orleans for being drunk and disorderly. The reporter painted Rafael Perdido as a mean-tempered, shiftless drifter, strictly out for himself.

It stated that he was found holding Camille Gravier's lifeless body at the edge of Moon Lake, where he'd supposedly strangled her. He had been discovered by Charles Delacroix and his sister, Mary. At the time, both men had been taken into custody and questioned, because they had both been in the water. Delacroix was later released, after his sister explained that he had gone into the lake in an attempt to save Camille. In fact, he was not only released, but later testified as a witness for the prosecution.

Mary Delacroix had also been a witness. One of the articles mentioned that Mary Delacroix and Camille had been close friends. In fact, Mary was so distraught over discovering the brutal murder of her friend that the day she took the witness stand to testify, she broke down completely and had to be carried from the courtroom. She didn't return to testify in person, but did so through a deposition. As soon as the trial ended she had gone to the south of France for almost a year in order to rest and recover.

Charles Delacroix, on the other hand, had willingly testified that he and Camille had been dating for several weeks. They had gone to the lake after taking in a movie that night in Covington. Charles had excused himself and gone into the woods for a few minutes, then he'd heard Camille scream. When he came running back he found Perdido holding Camille down in the water. "Young Delacroix made a valiant attempt to save Miss Gravier, but alas, he was too late," the article stated.

Perdido claimed that he had been out walking and heard a woman scream. He ran toward the lake, and when he got there, Camille Gravier was floating facedown. He ran into the water to rescue her, and Delacroix showed up just as he was trying to pull Camille out of the lake.

The prosecution contended that Perdido had made repeated attempts to get Camille to go out with him, but she had refused. Mary Delacroix's deposition supported that contention, stating that her friend had told her of Perdido's pursuit, and that he had cornered her one night, then kissed her, and "become offensive with his attentions." The testimony of the two Delacroix, combined with Perdido's record, gave the district attorney a solid case. The jury was out for only three hours and twenty-six minutes before they returned a guilty verdict. Rafael Perdido was sentenced to hang, and sent to Angola Prison.

And through the entire trial Hamilton Delacroix had defended the young drifter as brilliantly as expected. He had countered the prosecution's claims with plausible explanations, but in the end he had been defeated by technicalities in the form of rulings handed down by Judge Alvarez. In fact, it almost

looked as if the judge was an enemy of Hamilton
Delacroix rather than a friend, and was making him
pay through his client. Alvarez's rulings against the
defendant were frequent. Delacroix had objected just
as frequently, but to no avail.

Stunned, Travis stared at the faxes. None of what
he had just read fit with Camille's letters, or what
Gran had told him. None of it made sense. Something
was missing, and he intended to find out what. He
left the motel and drove straight to the courthouse in
Covington, which was the seat of St. Tammany parish
government. If he was lucky, maybe an old transcript
of the trial existed. Travis didn't care if he had to
spend the rest of the day dealing with bureaucratic
red tape and half of the night digging through dusty
boxes, he'd do whatever it took. If that failed, he
would recheck the old newspaper files. Foster must
have overlooked something, Travis decided. That had
to be the answer.

The red tape wasn't thick, but his success was limited. Transcripts of trials that old were stored on microfiche, and to have them made into a hard copy
would take at least ten days. Frustrated, Travis headed
for the newspaper's morgue.

And found more than he bargained for.

"Excuse me. You in charge of the morgue?" he
asked the elderly clerk sweeping the dusty basement.

"I reckon so, seeing how there's nobody else
here."

"I'm trying to get copies of newspaper articles on
a murder trial that took place in July 1938."

The old man peered over his bifocals. "What you
wanna go digging around that kinda mess for? Nice
young fella like you."

"Research for a book."

"Must be one of those gory things about famous murders. Well, you want gory, we got gory. Follow me," he told Travis, and propped his broom in a corner.

"Have you been in charge of these files for long?"

"Twenty-two years come next month. 'Fore that, I was a janitor at the newspaper for over forty years. Call it maintenance now."

"Were you around here in 1938?"

"Yes sir-ree bob. Sparkin' a real sweet little ole gal over in Slidell. Married her."

"Maybe you remember the Gravier murder."

"Not likely to forget it. Worst thing ever happened in St. Tammany parish at the time." The old clerk pointed to a table in a corner with an ancient microfiche viewer on top. "Take your time," he said, and walked away.

An hour later the caretaker poked his head in the door. "Going to lunch now. You gonna stay?"

Travis rubbed the back of his neck. "No." He turned off the machine. The articles were the same as the faxes from Foster. Nothing new.

"She was real pretty, that Gravier girl," the clerk said as they walked back into the basement office.

Travis's head snapped up. "You knew her?"

"Not personal. I knew the judge, though. Him and Hamilton Delacroix was buddies."

"Buddies?"

"Thick as thieves. Well, they was just about the two richest men in the parish then, I reckon, so figures they'd be friends. Guess you might say they traveled in the same circles. Their families even went to Europe together the year before the trial. You want to look at anything else?''

''No,'' Travis said, realizing he was walking away with more questions than answers. ''I'm done.''

He made one last stop at the Covington library, but came away empty-handed except for one thing. With the help of the librarian he learned that unless the cause of death was unknown, autopsies weren't performed in 1938. Not in rural Louisiana. That meant no one had known about Camille's pregnancy. Except possibly the father. But what if she'd been killed before she got a chance to tell Delacroix about the baby? Then again, an unwanted pregnancy was certainly a motive for murder. But Delacroix had admitted, under oath, that he was in love with Camille and had even considered marriage. If that was the case, he had no reason to kill her.

And what about Mary Delacroix? Had Camille confided in her best friend about being pregnant? And had Mary kept the secret, knowing it might incriminate her brother? Was it possible she had perjured herself to save Charles? And what about the judge's rulings? Given the good-old-boy system that undoubtedly existed in a rural community such as Bayou Beltane at that time, Travis found it odd that the reverse wasn't the case. Why hadn't Alvarez given his friend the benefit of the doubt?

Despite the information he had gained, Travis felt he was no closer to the truth about his great-aunt's death than when he'd come to Louisiana. Clearly the newspaper reporter had been biased, but somewhere, someone had to know the facts, and Travis vowed he would get them. Even if he had to go to Charles Delacroix himself.

That thought reminded him of the first time he'd laid eyes on Shelby.

*Sweet Shelby.*

She was the best—and worst—thing that had happened to him in years. And he was damned if he knew what to do about her. About his feelings for her. Try as he might, he couldn't deny that he *had* feelings. He thought about the implications and the complications of that fact as he drove back to Bayou Beltane.

BY THE TIME the secretary showed Walter Trowbridge into her office around three that afternoon, Shelby was ready for him.

"Ms. Delacroix." He smiled warmly. "So nice to meet you. Of course, I've known your family for years. By the way, congratulations on your father's appointment. Justin is a credit to our profession."

"Thank you." Despite the smile, Trowbridge didn't give off friendly vibes, and he had one of those faces that was difficult to read. Friendly vibes? Shelby smiled to herself. She'd been listening to Marie too long. The next thing Shelby knew, she would be wondering about his aura.

She gestured toward a chair. "Won't you have a seat?"

Trowbridge's backside had barely touched the chair before his briefcase was open and he was handing her documents. "Copies of the petition for determination of paternity and the petition for determination of custody. I assume Miss Avenall told you she received her copies yesterday?"

"*Ms.* Avenall did inform me." Shelby thought she saw annoyance flicker in the lawyer's eyes, but so briefly she couldn't be sure. But she knew for certain he was making a subtle attempt, even by address, to insinuate that her client was unmarried, therefore Dante was without a father figure.

"I can assure you that my client has no ill feelings toward Miss Avenall, and only wants what is best for his son."

"You mean *Ms.* Avenall's son. Paternity is yet to be determined."

"Yes, of course." The smile was back, but slightly stiffer. "But my client doesn't deny he's the father."

"Really."

"Let's talk plain, shall we, Ms. Delacroix?"

"By all means," Shelby said, knowing full well that was the last thing he intended to do. Now would begin the sparring match as they tested how strong a case each had.

"As I said, my client holds no ill feelings, but he must think about the welfare of his...the boy. After all, raising children is an expensive proposition, and your client is hardly financially secure. On the other hand, my client—"

"We're not questioning Mr. Masson's ability to provide food and clothing for a child. My question is can he provide a loving environment? After all, he did abandon Ms. Avenall *and* her son for over five years."

"On the contrary. Your client disappeared. Mr. Masson had no knowledge of the pregnancy."

"You'll have to prove that."

Trowbridge's smile had turned plastic. "Certainly. And I expect we'll have no shortage of folks willing to testify as to my client's sterling character."

"No doubt." Now she did see the annoyance in the lawyer's eyes. He knew she was inexperienced, and probably expected to find her nervous about dealing with a man of Lyle Masson's stature. But if Trowbridge knew her family as well as he claimed to, then he should have known the Delacroix were not easily rattled, young or old. Her grandfather and father had schooled her in the fine art of poker faces and professional attitudes from the time she was big enough to pull her first law book from a shelf. And if Trowbridge thought she was too young to handle this case, again he was short on knowledge.

"Your client, on the other hand, has, shall we say, a slight tarnish to her character."

He was baiting her, but Shelby didn't bite.

"You and Miss Avenall went to high school together, didn't you?"

"Yes."

"Kept in close contact, have you? I mean, you were away at law school for so long... I'm sure your friend was a sweet young thing when you knew her, but people do change."

Shelby was getting an uneasy feeling. The accusation about Yvette's past connection to prostitution was in the filed petition, so there was no surprise there. But he was heading somewhere with this line of talk. Either he was stringing her along, hoping she would say something he could use, or he knew something she didn't.

"My client is prepared to make Miss Avenall a very generous offer that will cover all back child support and will provide her with an, shall we say, easier life."

Shelby had expected the deal, had even anticipated that they would dress it up as child support, but she was a little surprised he had gotten to it so quickly. "In exchange for what?"

"Waiving all her parental rights."

Shelby's expression didn't alter. "Out of the question."

The smile was back. "Don't be so eager to turn down the offer, Ms. Delacroix. I'm trying to save you a good deal of public embarrassment, not to mention avoid a nick in this prestigious firm's reputation."

More nasty innuendos. She refused to let her anger surface. "I appreciate your concern, Mr. Trowbridge. And of course, I will take your offer to my client, but I feel certain her position on this matter will remain unchanged. She has no intention of relinquishing her parental rights. Now or ever."

"Did your client explain the circumstances under which she met Mr. Masson?"

"Yes."

"Mr. Masson wants this to be as painless as possible. He has no interest in causing your client undue harm. He's well aware that he stepped outside the bounds of his marriage by consorting with—"

"I believe they *dated* for over a year."

"In any event, he admits his error in judgment. As a matter of fact, he and Mrs. Masson have weathered the news of the boy's existence beautifully. They have a solid marriage and are prepared to offer a loving home. As I said, he bears your client no ill feelings. He's willing to offer a settlement that will enable Miss Avenall to attend college, if she so desires. Out of state, of course. Or, if she prefers, he's willing to help establish her in a business of her own."

"She already has a business of her own."

"So she does. A bookstore. Purchased, I believe,

with funds bequeathed her by a Mr. Paul Anderson of New Orleans. Her former...employer.''

He might as well have said lover straight out. The implication was crystal clear.

''Well.'' With his smug little smile in place, Walter Trowbridge closed his briefcase and stood up. ''Give our offer some thought, Ms. Delacroix.''

Shelby wanted to pick up the brass paperweight on her desk and throw it at him, but she refused to give him the satisfaction of even the slightest hesitation. ''Thank you. I will.'' When he turned to walk away, she waited until he was almost at the door, then stood up. ''Oh, Mr. Trowbridge, perhaps you could help me with one minor thing.''

''Certainly.''

''Were the two men that delivered Ms. Avenall's copies employed by your firm?''

''Why do you ask?''

She shrugged. ''Knowing your firm's reputation, you might want to revise your hiring criteria. At least impart to your staff a clear explanation of the penalty for harassment, possibly even bribery.''

''Thank you.''

''You're very welcome.''

The minute the door closed behind him, Shelby took a deep, cleansing breath. Good Lord, what had possessed her to tweak the nose of her opponent like that? Pride, of course. She couldn't stand the thought of him walking out of her office thinking he had gotten the best of her.

The trouble was, he had.

Either Trowbridge was bluffing, or Yvette had accidentally on purpose forgotten to mention that her retired former employer had left her a bundle. As lies of omission went, it was a whopper. Shelby snatched up the phone and punched in her friend's number, then hung up before it could ring. No. She needed to see Yvette's face when she asked her. Then she would know if she was lying.

Shelby notified the receptionist that she was leaving for the day, then grabbed her purse and briefcase. Ten minutes later she pulled up in front of the Book Nook.

Yvette was with a customer, the only customer, when Shelby walked in. She had to admit Yvette had done a nice job, arranging two or three areas among the shelves where customers could sit and read if they desired. There was also a small table set up near the cash register with complimentary coffee. Shelby browsed until the customer left, then walked up to Yvette.

"I need to ask you a question."

Yvette blinked at Shelby's crisp tone. "All right."

"Where did you get the money to set up this bookstore?"

"I—I...most people get loans—"

"Did you?"

"No, I—"

"Did you use the money Paul Anderson left you in his will?"

"Yes," she admitted, then rushed to add, "Paul was like a father to me, and he had no family."

"And the relationship was never anything more than platonic?"

All the color drained out of Yvette's face. "I—I...don't understand."

For the first time since spotting Yvette outside her office, Shelby felt a twinge of distrust. It made her mad—at Yvette and at herself. "Then, let me make it simple. Were you Paul Anderson's lover?"

Yvette's eyes filled with tears. "Shelby…"

"Oh, Lord," Shelby said, seeing the truth in her client's eyes.

Now the tears flowed freely. "It's not the way it sounds. We never…it wasn't the way it was with Lyle. Paul was so lonely, and he was good to Dante and me. I barely remember my own father, and Paul was… He loved me, but it was never…sex. Oh, God, Shelby, you've got to believe that."

"Of course I do," Shelby said without hesitation.

At that, Yvette broke down completely, sobs racking her slender body.

Shelby blew out a breath. "You should have told me, that's all," she said, slipping an arm around her friend's shoulders and drawing her into a comforting embrace. "You just should have told me."

The information was damaging, but it would be up to her to prove it wasn't damning. For the first time, Shelby felt the considerable weight of taking on this complicated case. As she patted Yvette's shoulder, she suddenly wished Travis were here. She felt safe when she was with him. And protected. Right now, she would like nothing better than so see him walk through the door to comfort her.

TRAVIS TOLD HIMSELF to keep on driving when he saw the exit for Bayou Beltane. He told himself that if he was smart he would go right back to his motel in Slidell and forget about the fact that he had promised to call Shelby. The problem was, of course, that he hadn't been smart about any of his involvement with Shelby from the beginning. And today didn't seem to be the day to start. He exited Interstate 12 and headed for Shelby's office, but was barely into town when he spotted her little red sports car parked in front of the Book Nook. He pulled in beside her car and got out. Travis wasn't exactly sure what he expected to find when he stepped inside. Truthfully, he wasn't exactly sure why he had felt compelled to stop in the first place.

When he opened the door and heard sobs coming from the other side of a rack of books, he thought for a heart-stopping moment that it was Shelby. Then he heard her voice.

"Now, you listen to me. We're going to fight Masson every inch of the way. He's not going to get his hands on your son if I have anything to say about it. Do you hear me?"

He heard a sniffing sound, then a faint, "Yes."

"Trust me?"

"Yes" came the answer, stronger this time.

Deciding he was intruding, Travis was in the process of backing quietly out the door when Shelby and a blond woman appeared from among the shelves.

"Travis!" Shelby said, totally surprised to see her wish materialize in the flesh.

"I was just coming into town and I, uh, saw your car... You're busy, so I'll call you—"

"No, wait." She glanced at the woman beside her and spoke in hushed tones. The woman looked at Travis, her blue eyes red-rimmed from crying, then she hurried off toward the back of the store.

"Is she okay?" Travis asked as the woman disappeared.

Shelby gazed up at him. "Yes. At least, she will be."

"Didn't mean to interrupt."

"It's all right."

"Are you…" She was looking at him so strangely. "Are you sure?"

"Yes. But in the future, I need to be careful what I wish for."

"Care to translate, darlin'?"

"A few minutes ago I wished you would walk though the door and—" she shrugged "—here you are."

He grinned, trying to ignore the way her honesty tugged at his guilt. "Guess that means you've got two wishes left."

She reached out and took his hand. "I'm really glad you're here."

He could see she wasn't going to let him off the hook no matter how hard he tried to keep things impersonal. His only defense was to move on. "Are you going back to your office?"

"No. I thought I might go for a ride. Would you like to join me?"

Suddenly the idea of flying across the countryside astride a horse sounded like exactly the tonic he needed after the day he'd had. He didn't want to think about all the questions with no answers, all the doubts.

"You think you've got an animal out there among all those fancy Thoroughbreds that won't turn up his nose at an ole Texas cowboy?"

"Oh, I think we can find a horse that's not prejudiced."

"In that case, you're on."

The smile she gave him shamed the sun. For the

first time in his life he truly understood what the word *radiant* meant.

"Why don't you follow me to Riverwood?"

"Yeah," Travis said, knowing each of her smiles was harder to resist than the last. "Why don't I?"

SOMEWHERE BETWEEN the Book Nook and Riverwood, Shelby discovered that Travis Hardin had become very important to her. Actually, the discovery had come when she looked up and saw him standing in the doorway of the bookstore. She couldn't quite explain it, but in that instant her relationship with Travis changed. At least on her part. She wasn't superstitious, and she didn't believe in magic, white or black, but somehow she felt his appearance at the bookstore was a sign that it was time for her to risk loving again. Not that she had any real choice, because she was very much afraid she was falling in love with him. She had admitted her attraction, but until today she hadn't actually allowed herself to believe it could be more. And it was. Much more.

She wasn't so hopelessly naive that she expected the same kind of feelings from Travis. He was trying to keep his distance, that much she knew. But why? Maybe he had been hurt before. Or maybe he didn't want to hurt her. Was that it? She had said it herself— he was only in town for a short while, and maybe he was trying to avoid getting her hopes up for anything other than a brief fling. Maybe. But if her instincts were right, she didn't think it was that simple.

Whatever it was, she knew one thing for sure— seeing him in the doorway to the bookstore had sent a clear message: no risk, no reward.

## *CHAPTER EIGHT*

TRAVIS WAS HALFWAY through saddling a bay named
Lord Byron when he felt someone watching him. He
glanced at Shelby saddling her own horse in the next
stall, but she was focused on the horse, not him. Then
he turned around. A man, Native American from the
look of his bone structure, not to mention a mane of
silver hair held back by a beaded headband, was
watching him intently.

"Travis," Shelby said, walking around the end of
the stall. "This is Robert Bearclaw. Bear, meet Travis
Hardin."

Travis offered his hand. "Pleasure to meet you."

"You looked at Zaira," Bear said as he shook
hands.

Travis nodded. "Fine animal."

"She'll have strong foals. You planning on buying
her?"

"Could be. I haven't made up my mind just yet."

"It's good to wait. Sometimes quick decisions
bring regret." Bear's gaze drilled him, then slid to
Shelby, leaving little doubt in Travis's mind that the
Indian had just delivered a message. It was almost as
if Bear knew Travis wasn't simply who he said he
was. But how could he?

"Bear knows every horse on the place. He helped
bring most of them into the world. And he can pick

potential winners practically before they can stand on their wobbly little legs."

"Mr. Bearclaw's reputation has traveled all the way to Texas. As I said, it's a pleasure, sir."

"And I've seen you twice in as many days," Bear said to Shelby. "Does these old eyes good."

Shelby smiled. "Old eyes, my foot. You see everything that goes on around here."

His gaze swung from Shelby to Travis and stayed, intensified. "I see a lot."

Travis got the message loud and clear.

"Well," Shelby said, taking her horse's reins. "You're about to see us ride out of here."

Travis followed her, leading Lord Byron, but he could feel Robert Bearclaw's gaze all the way out of the stables. The old Indian was watching him like a farmer protecting a henhouse.

"Don't mind Bear," Shelby told him. "He's protective of all of us. Like a nanny with an attitude."

Shelby was making light of the way Bear sized up what he probably thought was the intruder from Texas, but Travis was still uneasy. Maybe the Indian was just looking out for a Delacroix daughter. Or maybe, Travis decided, the uneasiness stemmed from his own guilty conscience. Three days ago his intentions had been clear, his determination unshakable: nothing was going to get in the way of uncovering the truth about Camille Gravier's death.

But Shelby had got in the way.

And every time he saw her, he drew closer to her and further from his mission of revenge.

"Ready, Travis?"

Standing beside his horse, he looked up and found

Shelby already mounted. "Yeah." He stepped up into the saddle and followed her lead.

They rode south through a sparse pine forest parallel to a narrow bayou, then crossed over the road leading northwest out of Bayou Beltane. They rode for a half hour, eventually making a wide arc, crossing back over the road and heading once again toward Riverwood.

Travis had a hard time keeping his mind on the animal beneath him, because he couldn't stop looking at Shelby. The wind tousled her hair; the sun kissed her cheeks as she and her horse moved in graceful unity. He had never seen anything so beautiful in his entire life. The thought crossed his mind to sweep her off her horse and into his arms. Then he'd just keep on riding, leaving everything behind and heading off into the sunset like in an old movie. It wasn't reality, but watching Shelby made him wish it was.

Finally, skirting the exercise track, they galloped across a bridge over the bayou on the east side of the breeding farm.

"Race you to that stand of pines," Shelby called, and instantly kicked her mount into a full gallop. But Travis was quicker than she expected, and they barreled toward the trees neck and neck, reining in their horses within seconds of each other.

"That was great," she said, swinging out of the saddle.

Travis tied both horses to a nearby tree. "Darlin', I hope you're not about to get us arrested for trespassing."

"Arrested?"

He pointed to a house on the other side of the trees about five hundred yards away, but easily in view.

"Heavens, no. That's just my aunt Mary and uncle William's house."

"Tell me something—is there *any* land around here that doesn't belong to the Delacroix?"

"Sure," she said with a laugh. "The newer section of town on the other side of I-12. Most of that has been bought up by developers."

"New money, huh? No class," he said, teasing.

"Hey, I can't help it if my family owns half of the parish. Personally, I couldn't afford to invest in one square yard of real estate if I wanted to. I did that once and almost lost my shirt."

"You may not be a real estate tycoon, darlin', but you'd make a damned good barrel racer. You dodged those trees like a pro."

"I should. I've covered every inch of this ground on horseback ever since I was a kid."

"Hell, no wonder you were so quick to race. You'd hedged your bet. In fact—" he came toward her wearing a decidedly wicked smile and matching gleam in his eyes "—I might think you cheated."

"Careful, cowboy." She took a step back, then bent and scooped up a handful of pinecones from the carpet of needles underfoot. "My sister's a cop and my daddy's a judge." She lobbed the first cone, yelping with satisfaction when it hit Travis squarely in the chest.

"Oh, darlin', you're going to pay for that." He took off after her.

Shelby squealed and ran, occasionally tossing pinecones as she darted through the trees to avoid capture. Travis aimed a couple of cones at her fanny as she changed direction and ran back toward the horses. Again he was quicker than she expected. As she neared her horse, intending to make good her escape, he caught her around the waist and spun her around. The momentum of the capture tipped them both off balance, and they went down in a tangle of arms and legs. At the last second, Travis twisted so that his body took the brunt of the fall. Shelby landed on top of him.

"That was fun!" she exclaimed, laughing and panting at the same time.

"You attacked me."

"Did not. Besides, you deserved it for saying I cheated." She doubled up her fist and pretended to clip his jaw.

He grabbed her hand and their gazes met. Whatever he had been about to say simply evaporated from his brain. He couldn't think when she was this close. When she smelled like sunshine and felt like heaven.

"Are you going to kiss me?" she asked breathlessly.

"Looks that way."

"Good."

He lifted his head and fitted his mouth to hers. And in an instant, laughter gave way to lust, fun to friction—the kind of reaction that sizzles, sings through the blood and makes it burn.

Sprawled on top of him, Shelby gave no thought to how heavy she might be. She gave no thought to the fact that they were clearly visible to anyone taking the road to Aunt Mary's house. The only thing she thought about was the flavor and feel of Travis. He tasted like excitement. He felt like power. Both were dangerous, both seductive. Feeling reckless, she tightened her hands in his hair and deepened the kiss, telling him in no uncertain terms that she recognized and welcomed the heat shimmering through their bodies.

His attempt at control was weak at best, and he realized he wanted this, needed it. The only thing that made any sense in the whole Delacroix debacle was Shelby. Sweet, warm Shelby. He kept reminding himself that she was delicate, like a fine porcelain teacup that had to be handled with care. It helped to keep him sane. It helped to keep him from ripping her clothes off her delicate body and making them both wild with need. But when she pulled herself a little higher on his body and rocked against him, he didn't think he could stand it. When she groaned in pleasure at the first stroke of his tongue, the leash on his control almost snapped. He struggled, caught in a tug of war between what he wanted, and what he knew was right. Between desire and the determination to stay free of whatever spell she seemed to have cast over him. In the end, want and desire were too strong. Rolling to his side, he took her with him. Settling her on her back, he hooked his foot over hers as if to hold her there.

Shelby wasn't going anywhere. She was right where she wanted to be. "Wow," she whispered when they broke the kiss. She slid an arm around his neck but made no move to kiss him again. "You know what's going to happen if you stay in Bayou Beltane much longer, don't you?"

He knew. But for some reason he wanted to hear her say it. Wanted to hear her say that she wanted him. "Maybe you better spell it out."

"We're going to end up in a tangle of arms and legs and wild kisses."

He glanced down at their bodies pressed together

on the sweet-smelling pine needles. "I hate to state the obvious, darlin', but that's pretty much where we are now."

"Yeah, but we've got our clothes on."

Travis gazed at her mouth, still moist from his kiss. "Trust me. At the moment, no one's more aware of that than I am."

She smiled. "Then I guess it's safe to assume that you want me."

Leaning into her, pressing the hard ridge of his arousal against her hip, he chuckled. "Hardly a news flash, darlin'."

"I want you, too." She stroked his cheek, the tenderness of the gesture more jolting than their rampant desire. "And the rules haven't changed, Travis."

"Rules?"

"No orange blossoms. No undying promises. In my clumsy way, I'm trying to tell you that I want to make love with you, but it doesn't mean you owe me anything."

There was nothing clumsy about her. In fact, he was totally awed that this beautiful, honest woman wanted him. As far as owing her anything went, in his heart he knew he owed her the truth.

"Before you say anything," she added hastily, "I think there's something you should know. I haven't…what I mean is, it's been a while since I've been with a man, so I may not…" She took a breath and released it slowly. "I'm making a real mess of this."

God, she was offering herself to him with both hands. How was he supposed to turn away from such sweetness when the truth was he didn't want to?

"I've embarrassed you, haven't I?" she asked him.

"No."

"Shocked you?"

"No. I just can't figure why some man hasn't come along and snapped you up."

"Maybe because I wasn't interested."

"Why?" he blurted without thinking.

"No one has ever turned me on the way you do."

"No one?"

She moved her head from side to side. "Not until I turned around and saw you standing beside me day before yesterday."

"Shelby—"

"If you're going to say this has all happened too fast, you're right. Maybe I shouldn't say how much I want you. Maybe slow and easy is better, but it's not the way I feel."

"Shelby—"

She put her finger against his lips to silence what she suspected was a logical protest. "Travis, there're no strings attached. No obligations. And like you said, I'm a grown-up. I can take rejection."

"I...I don't know what to say."

"Say you'll think about it?"

He cupped her chin in his hand while his thumb skimmed across her bottom lip. "I haven't thought about much else since I met you."

She closed her eyes briefly and smiled. "Kiss me again," she whispered.

He wanted to go slow, to give back the tenderness she had shown him, but when his mouth touched hers, her breathless murmur for more had need twisting sharply in his gut. As her lips parted beneath his, he deepened the kiss until he felt the thud of her heart beating against his chest. Desire ripped through him.

Tremors, delicious tremors, expanded through Shelby's body like ripples in a pond, moving, growing wider, stronger. She gave up any thought of control and discovered all remnants of fear went with it. Her only regret was that they weren't someplace that afforded them more privacy.

As if he had read her mind, Travis drew back to look at her. Her lips were swollen and moist, her eyes half-closed and dazed with desire. And he was so close to taking her, it scared him.

"Probably wouldn't look good—" resting his forehead on hers, he tried to steady his breathing "—for a lawyer to be arrested for indecent exposure, huh?"

"Probably not," she said, equally as breathless. "When I make it to the Supreme Court I'll see what I can do about getting rid of such silly laws."

A chuckle started deep in his chest and rumbled into a full laugh. Gently, he rolled over to lie beside her. "I'm not sure I'll last that long."

"Any man who survives the Catfish Shack has got more stamina than he realizes."

They lay on the ground for several minutes, then finally Travis got to his feet and offered her a hand up. "Hold still," he said when they were both standing.

"What?"

"You've got some stuff..." He plucked several pine needles from her hair.

"Oh." She removed a few herself. "All gone?"

"Think so."

Shelby ran her fingers through her hair, then shook her head to be certain. When she lifted her head, her dark hair was as wildly tousled as that of a gypsy princess, her smile as mysterious.

"C'mon." He took her hand and they started toward the horses. "We better get outta here while I've still got my sanity," he said.

"You mean you don't want a chance to get even for losing the race?"

"I'd just as soon walk for a while if it's all the same to you, darlin'."

"Why?" she asked, before she realized the obvious answer. Automatically, her gaze dropped to the front of his jeans, then darted away. "Oh. Sure."

Travis grinned. Sassy one minute, stunningly candid the next, and wide-eyed and a little innocent a second after that, Shelby was a delightful combination. "So tell me," he said as they led their horses toward the bridge, "how many Delacroix were probably watching us through the window of that house a few minutes ago?"

Shelby groaned. "Only two, but they carry a lot of weight in our family. Aunt Mary and Uncle William live there."

It was all Travis could do not to turn and stare at the place. Mary Delacroix. Camille's closest friend. He would give anything to have just five minutes with her.

"Neither of them has ever married. Aunt Mary—actually, she's my great-aunt—celebrated her eightieth birthday a couple of months ago, and her brother, my great-uncle William, is a retired priest. Lord only knows what they thought if they *did* see us."

"Trouble?"

"Not really. Uncle William is the most gentle, understanding man I have ever known. But Aunt Mary…"

"Straitlaced?"

Frowning, Shelby shook her head. "No, she's terrific, but her heart isn't strong. The doctors say she'll be okay, but they've advised her to avoid any stress, physical or emotional. She's really special, and we all love her dearly. I wouldn't like to think I was responsible for causing her any sort of shock."

"Of course not." Talking to Mary Delacroix didn't seem like such a good idea, all at once. "If it makes you feel better, I really don't think anyone could see us from the house."

"Probably not."

As much as he would like to know more about his own great-aunt and her murder, causing Shelby's aging relative undue stress wasn't something Travis wanted on his conscience. He'd have to find someone else to talk to, another way to get information.

Meanwhile, the woman walking beside him was becoming as necessary as air. If things were different, if he had met her somewhere else, or another time... But things weren't different, and he was here now, facing a dilemma that was partly of his own making, partly circumstantial. What was he going to do?

The simple answer was to go back to Texas and leave Dale Foster to ferret out the facts, but Travis had resisted doing that from the beginning. Truthfully, his reasons for staying had changed because of Shelby.

"How much longer will you be staying?" she asked as they walked the horses across the wooden bridge. "I don't mean to pry, I was just—"

"You weren't. I plan on looking at a couple more mares. Suppose I need to make a decision soon."

"Tomorrow is Saturday."

Travis smiled. "Is that a fact?"

"I don't have to work."

"You know, I think that's a subtle hint."

She nudged him. "I do love a man who's quick."

"All right. Tomorrow we go shopping for a mare. Guess that means you'll have to put up with me for a while longer."

Shelby stopped walking and gazed up at him, serious now. "You know, if you hang around for a while, we might get all tangled up."

He knew she was talking about limbs and lips, and that she had no idea how tangled things already were. She had no idea what a hold she already had on his heart.

"I'll risk it if you will, darlin'."

They walked on to the stables, handed their horses over to a groom, then headed toward the house. The sun was slipping toward sunset, and Travis was just about to say goodbye to Shelby when Charles Delacroix stepped out onto the wide front porch.

"Good evening, Mr. Hardin."

"Mr. Delacroix."

"How was your ride?" Charles asked Shelby.

"Thrilling."

"Good. I was a little concerned at first, since it's getting on toward suppertime, but Bear told me you were with Mr. Hardin."

"Travis, sir." As much as Travis disliked being friendly toward Charles, the man was Shelby's granddaddy and it was silly to stay so formal.

"Thank you, Travis. Jax tells me you're checking out our competition."

"Yes, sir."

"Smart. But I hope that doesn't mean you've ruled out Zaira."

"Absolutely not. In fact, I've decided to buy her. And I've also decided to purchase another mare before I head back to Texas."

"Have you, indeed? Well, we welcome the chance to compete for additional business. I was beginning to think your interest might have switched from horses to pretty young lawyers."

Charles's smile was polite, and his voice was pleasant enough, but Travis had the feeling the old man would just as soon see the last of him. For good.

"Our Shelby's quite a charmer, you know."

"Oh, Granddad." Shelby blushed.

"Why, that's only the truth, my dear. I was afraid you had stolen Travis's heart and toyed with his affections."

Or the other way around, Travis thought. The message was clear. In his subtle, Southern way, Charles was letting the upstart from the other side of the Mississippi River know not to trifle with Delacroix women.

"Please, Granddad. You make me sound like Scarlett O'Hara."

"Nonsense, child." He took her hand and slipped it through his arm. With Shelby on his arm as if he had reclaimed her, Charles looked at Travis. "We're about to have our evening meal. Would you do us the honor of joining us?"

For a second Travis almost refused, then he changed his mind—partly because he wanted to spend more time with Shelby and partly because he thought Charles Delacroix wanted and expected him to decline. "Thank you, sir. I'd like that very much."

The flash of annoyance in the old man's eyes was

so brief Travis almost didn't catch it. He was grateful Shelby missed it.

"Is Jax joining us?" she asked.

"I believe so. And William, as well."

"Great. I can't wait for you to meet Uncle William, Travis. He's a sweetheart."

"I'm looking forward to it."

"Well," Charles said, "shall we go in?"

WITH THE EXCEPTION of Shelby, William was the most pleasant Delacroix Travis had met. The retired priest was warm and engaging, sharing stories both humorous and touching about the people in his parish.

"So, Mr. Hardin—"

"Travis, sir."

"Only if you drop the sir."

Travis smiled. "Deal."

"So, Travis. My brother tells me that you're from Texas?"

"Yes. A little town called Comfort. It's not far from San Antonio."

William smiled broadly. "San Antonio is a lovely city. Many years ago I attended a two-day conference there." He patted his slightly rounded middle. "Incredible food."

"Some of the best in the state."

"I took a tour of the Alamo. You know, it's one thing to read about battles, but totally another thing to actually tread the ground where brave men died. The experience was moving. I've never forgotten it."

"Uncle William is sort of our family historian," Shelby said. "He's documented it back more than a hundred years. Anything you want to know about us, he's the man to ask."

"Really?" *Finally,* Travis thought. If William was the man with all the answers, he was definitely the man Travis wanted to talk to. Privately, of course. Just how he could do that without arousing suspicion, he wasn't sure, but he would find a way.

"Not only has he compiled the history of the Delacroix," Shelby added, "but he's also considered to be quite a local historian. He knows just about everything that has gone on in Bayou Beltane since its beginning."

Travis sipped the white wine served with the delicious shrimp dish and yearned for an ice cold long neck. "So you're the man with all the answers."

"I wouldn't go that far."

"With all the Civil War battles that took place in Louisiana, that must be an interesting hobby."

"It's been an interest of mine for many years. Before I retired, it was a hobby. Now it helps me fill days that were once filled with helping others."

"William, you make it sound like you spend all your time with your nose stuck in history books," Charles said. "Don't let his modesty fool you, Travis. He still does much more than his doctor would approve of, if he knew. I have it on good authority that the day before yesterday he was down on his knees helping one of his parishioners plant a garden."

"And what's wrong with a priest being on his knees?"

"Nothing, except when the priest has a touch of diabetes and failing eyesight. You could have fallen or Lord knows what."

"As indeed he does. Don't nag, Charles. I'm fine." William turned to Travis. "As you can see, lengthy history or not, we're no different from most families.

Of course, we've got a scoundrel or two in our past. But then, doesn't everyone?''

"Probably.'' Would the good father define *scoundrel* as "murderer,'' Travis wondered, if he knew about a certain juicy piece of Delacroix history? What would the family historian think of the fact that an innocent man had died for a crime the priest's own brother had committed?

"And speaking of scoundrels,'' William said, after swallowing a bite of the bread pudding Odelle had just served, "where is that great-nephew of mine? It was bad enough that Jax had to miss dinner because of one her horses. What happened to Beau?''

"Business,'' Charles answered. "He called at the last minute to say he had to go to Baton Rouge. Something he and Justin are involved in.''

"And what do you hear from Charlotte?''

Shelby bypassed the bread pudding for a helping of fresh fruit salad. "Charly says the police academy is a real killer. I was talking to her a few days ago.''

"And sweet Marie?''

Charles sighed. "Who knows about Marie? I don't understand all this—'' he waved his hand in the air "—all this voodoo.''

"Aromatherapy, Granddad. The voodoo items are for tourists.''

"Forgive us, Travis,'' William interjected. "We're such a scattered bunch these days that we have to constantly play catch-up regarding everyone's lives. We must be boring you.''

"Not at all.''

"William is right. Why don't we take our coffee into the parlor?'' Charles suggested.

Travis wiped his mouth with a linen napkin embroidered with the initial *D* and set it beside his plate. "Afraid I'm gonna have to call it a night." As much as he enjoyed William's company, he couldn't wait to be away from Charles.

"So soon?" Shelby asked.

"Yeah." He looked at Charles. "Thank you, sir, for inviting me to dinner. I enjoyed the meal very much."

"And we enjoyed having you, Travis."

"I'll walk you to your car." Before her grandfather could object, Shelby pushed away from the table and walked out of the room with Travis. "I can't blame you," she said once they were outside.

"For what?"

"Wanting to leave. All the family stuff can be a bit overpowering."

"Wasn't that—"

"Liar. You had to be dying to get out of there. I was."

Since he couldn't tell her the real reason he wanted to leave, the one she was after was as good as any. "I'm just not used to eating off fancy china, drinking out of crystal and using the good silver. Where I come from, darlin', good silver is used to fill cavities."

Laughing, Shelby looped her arms around his neck. "I'm awfully glad you came to town, Travis Hardin."

"Is that a fact?"

"Hmm. You're just want I need." Her laughter subsided as she gazed up at him. "Just what I need."

"If you keep talking like that, there's going to be trouble."

"Think so?"

"Yeah, because I'm going to have to kiss you."

"Sounds reasonable."

"Your granddaddy might not agree."

"Why? You planning on kissing him, too?"

Travis reached up and tugged on a lock of her hair. "Smart-ass."

"So I'm told. Smart enough to recognize a good thing when I see it." She rose up on her tiptoes and gave him a quick kiss. "What time are you picking me up tomorrow?"

"How about after breakfast? Say, nine-thirty?"

"Terrific. But I do have to run a quick errand to drop off some food."

"No problem, darlin'. Wherever you need to go."

"It's just over at Aunt Mary's."

IT DIDN'T TAKE A DOCTOR to see that Mary Delacroix wasn't feeling well that day. Perched on a chaise longue with a shawl across her shoulders, she looked pale and tired.

"Who's this ray of early morning sunshine I see?" she said as Shelby went over and kissed her cheek.

"Aunt Mary, I want you to meet a friend of mine, Travis Hardin. Travis, this wonderful woman is my aunt Mary."

"A pleasure, ma'am."

"Shelby's friends are always welcome. Do I detect a Texas drawl, Mr. Hardin?"

"Just plain Travis, and yes, ma'am." As he leaned over to shake her hand, he caught a faint scent of lavender. A childhood memory—of his grandmother sitting at her vanity dabbing the scent behind her ear—hit him like a smack in the face. Automatically, his hand jerked.

"I…excuse me. I didn't mean to startle you. That

fragrance was one my grandmother always wore, and it just reminded me of how much I miss her."

"Has her passing been recent?" Mary asked gently. "Oh, you poor boy," she said when he nodded. "I'm so sorry. Please accept my condolences."

"Thank you. Actually, you remind me of Gran in a lot of ways. Her hair was just about the same color, and she was soft-spoken, too." In fact, Mary Delacroix reminded him a lot of Gran. Probably neither woman would have been considered handsome, but they had a certain attraction, nonetheless. And then Travis realized what it was: natural beauty. Mary had the same joy, the same genuine concern for people as Shelby did. As Gran had had. That inner glow that always makes a woman beautiful.

"Well, I know this may sound silly, but you remind me of someone, too. Hardin…" Mary thought for a moment. "Do you have family in Louisiana, Travis?"

"No, ma'am."

"He did at one time. As matter of fact, he's poked around in some old records looking for information, but without much luck," Shelby said. "The name was Schmidt, wasn't it, Travis?"

"That's right."

"Oh, my, that was a rather common name in the parish forty or fifty years ago."

"It would take a little while to track, I'm afraid."

"Well, I regret you weren't able to connect with your past, but you certainly seem to have connected with my great-niece in the present."

"Aunt Mary, you're shameless," Shelby gently chided.

"When you say things like that at age twenty,

you're considered shameless. At my age, you're considered eccentric. Or senile. Besides, all I have to do is look at you to know you're very happy, and I wouldn't be a bit surprised if Travis wasn't partly responsible.''

Travis smiled. "Now I see where Shelby gets her charm. It runs in the family."

"Oh, I like him, Shelby."

"I thought you would. Listen," Shelby said, "while you two talk, I'll take this food into the kitchen. Odelle sends her love and prayers."

"Thank you, dear. And please give her my thanks for everything."

When Shelby left the room, Mary motioned to Travis. "Come here. No, closer, so I can get a real good look at you."

Travis went down on one knee so he and Mary were at eye level.

She studied him, cocking her head to one side, then the other, and for a moment he was afraid she might recognize something of his grandmother in him. He had always been told he had her eyes.

"You do look familiar. I must have known one of your people years ago, but for the life of me, I can't..." Her gaze intensified, then she sighed. "That's one of the worst things about growing old. My memory just isn't what it used to be."

"That happens to all of us once in a while."

She gave a little wave of dismissal. "No matter. What matters to me is the happiness of my family, and I can see that you make Shelby happy."

"I'm not sure—"

"Everyone will tell you I'm an outrageous matchmaker, and it's quite true. And I've been working on

Shelby for some time, but…'' Smiling, Mary reached out and took his hand. ''I think I can stop now.''

Travis had spent a precious few minutes in Mary Delacroix's presence, yet gazing into her eyes, he knew Shelby had gotten more than charm from her great-aunt. Here was the foundation of Shelby's honest, loving character. And he knew he had the answer to at least one of his questions.

Mary Delacroix could never lie.

He knew it, or maybe ''felt it'' was more accurate—the same way he'd felt the instant connection to Shelby. In fact, he wouldn't be surprised to learn that Mary had never told a lie in her life. The stunning impact of his realization was just hitting him when Shelby walked up behind him.

''Leave you with my beau for five minutes and you've got him down on one knee holding your hand,'' Shelby teased.

''The other way around, dear. *I* was holding *his* hand.''

''She's a real temptress,'' Travis said, standing.

''Don't I know it.''

''Oh, you two stop teasing an old woman and go have fun.''

Shelby kissed her great-aunt's cheek. ''Take care.''

Mary smiled up at Travis. ''Make Shelby bring you back for another visit.''

''I'd like that.'' He and Shelby turned to leave, then he stopped and looked back. ''It was a real honor to meet you, Mary.''

''Thank you. Now shoo, shoo,'' she said, waving them off.

As he helped Shelby into the front seat of his truck and walked around to the driver's side, Travis knew that the last half hour had changed the complexion of his revenge. To what extent, he wasn't sure. But one thing was certain, he needed to reevaluate things, and there was no way he could do that while he was with Shelby. He couldn't get out of the plans for today, but he had to put some distance between them.

"THANKS FOR BEING my guide," he told her. "I'd never have found a couple of those back road short-cuts." They had looked at two more mares and enjoyed lunch at a diner in Covington. After a long day's drive, they had reached Riverwood and were parked in the driveway.

"I enjoyed every minute. Do you have more appointments set up for tomorrow? I'd be happy to help."

"You're sweet, darlin', but you deserve some time off. I'm going over to a sale barn in Kenner, and maybe over around Houma. I'll give you a call tomorrow or the next day."

Surprised and a little hurt that he had made plans that didn't include her, Shelby wanted to ask why, but she restrained herself. Despite her feelings for him, she couldn't expect him to spend every minute with her. After all, he had come to Bayou Beltane on business, not pleasure. "Well, then," she said, sliding her arm around his neck. "I suppose you'd better kiss me good-night."

"Suppose I better," he agreed, and kissed her deeply.

# CHAPTER NINE

TRAVIS SPENT THE NEXT DAY and a half trying to accomplish two things: finding quality mares to buy and not thinking about meeting Mary Delacroix. He failed on both counts. None of the mares he looked at could hold a candle to Zaira, for one thing. And he couldn't reconcile what he thought was true with his gut instinct about Mary being so kind, caring and honest that she was nearly a saint. His plan for revenge had a serious hole in it.

But if Mary had told the truth sixty years ago, and Charles was innocent, then who had killed Camille? Perdido? Then why would Gran have insisted the wrong man had been convicted?

As Travis drove toward Slidell he thought about the evening ahead. He and Shelby had finally given up on dinner at Commander's Palace and instead had decided to do New Orleans impromptu. They planned to take in sunset by the Riverwalk, then let their appetites dictate the choice of a casual restaurant that didn't require reservations. They would finish off the evening at Chanson Triste, a blues club owned by Shelby's aunt Toni.

Travis checked his watch. If he moved fast he could shower and change, and he and Shelby could leave before six o'clock, the time his dad usually ended the workday. If Travis was lucky, he would miss another call. He had avoided talking to T.C. since meeting Mary, simply because he didn't know how to explain what was happening to their plan, much less what was happening to him.

Foster's report on Philip Delacroix had made for some interesting reading. It was clear to Travis that Philip was not only selfish and ruthless, but incredibly cunning. Not a man to be underestimated or crossed. And he ran with a group of men that were equally powerful and vicious—sharks with a Southern drawl. While Travis still wasn't willing to acquit Charles of Camille's murder despite what he had learned, he could say without hesitation that he'd deal with Charles over Philip any day.

Travis had only one untapped source left: William Delacroix.

Ever since he had learned that Shelby's great-uncle was the local historian, he had been trying to devise an "accidental" meeting in the hope of asking him some questions, but so far it hadn't worked. Travis had come to the conclusion that he would have to use a more direct approach.

Maybe William would be able to provide some missing elements. Travis had begun to think of all the information and clues he had collected as pieces of a gigantic jigsaw puzzle, with several vital sections missing. Try as he might, he couldn't make it all fit together. In fact, his brain hurt from trying. Tonight he wanted to be with Shelby and forget about murders, lies and promises.

Maybe he was kidding himself, but he had begun to believe that he and Shelby might have something together. She was everything he wanted in a woman. She was smart, funny, honest and loyal. And while he wouldn't alter any of those qualities, he knew her loyalty to her family would probably be the death of any relationship he hoped to have with her.

She had said it herself: nothing mattered like family. But she had also stated how much she hated injustice. Travis only hoped the two were not mutually exclusive, because he was dangerously close to falling in love with her.

IT WAS A PERFECT late afternoon in October, Shelby thought as she whipped her little red convertible through New Orleans traffic.

"I haven't done anything like this in ages," she told Travis.

"You mean chauffeur a handsome man around town?"

"I mean come to the city with a see-what-happens-and-just-go-for-it attitude."

"You gotta get out more, darlin'."

"Oh, I don't know." She glanced over at him and smiled. "Sometimes the nicest things happen in your own backyard."

The traffic became congested, slowing them to a crawl. "I knew there was a lot of construction going on, but I had no idea it was this bad," she continued. "At this rate we won't make it before Marie closes her shop. All right with you if we park a couple of blocks away and walk?"

"No problem, darlin'."

Shelby parked the convertible, got out, walked to the back and retrieved a box from the trunk.

"Aren't you going to put the top up?" Travis asked.

"Ever see a convertible top that could stand up to

a determined thief? The trunk is locked and the alarm system is state-of-the-art." She set the alarm and led Travis toward Jackson Square.

"There." She pointed as they turned onto St. Ann Street. "There's Marie's shop. It's called Heaven Scent."

Travis grinned. "Clever."

"So is Marie."

"Well, I'll say this. You Delacroix are an interesting bunch. Lawyers, judges, cops and even a—what did you call her?"

"Aromatherapist."

"Yeah, herbs and things, right?"

"It's more than just herbs, and Marie takes her work seriously. So do her clients."

"Clients?"

"Marie does therapeutic massage and offers alternative methods of healing, including herbal medicines. She has an extensive clientele."

Travis pointed to the sign in the window advertising voodoo charms. "Do any of her alternatives include potions and chicken parts?"

Shelby glanced over her shoulder and laughed. "Yes and no."

"Okay. Now you've got me curious." He took her arm. "Got any snakes or toads in that box?"

"You think you're joking, don't you?"

He stopped walking. "You pulling my leg?"

"Gotcha." Shelby grinned.

"Darlin', if that box moves," he quipped as he opened the door for her, "you're on your own."

Travis's first impression of Heaven Scent was that it reeked of sandalwood. The aroma had never appealed to him. That fact coupled with the array of strange paraphernalia displayed in the shop made him give the box in Shelby's hand another look. Then he peered at labels on some of the containers, fully expecting to read Eye of Newt or Lizard's Tongue. Just then a woman swept through a curtain of beads.

"Oh, good, you're here." She smiled and embraced Shelby.

"Sorry we're so late, but the construction is a mess. We had to park over on Dumaine Street."

"That's okay. I've got a customer who's absolutely dying for those herbs and…" She looked at Travis. "Oh, hello," she said.

The delicate young woman with the inquisitive expression on her face looked so much like Shelby there was no doubt they were sisters. Her hair was every bit as dark, with the same waves. In fact, except for the color of their eyes and the distinctive difference in their wardrobe styles, they could have been twins. Where Shelby tended more toward solid colors and classic lines, her sister went in for bright colors and lots of them, including a floral print scarf attractively tied around her head.

"Marie, this is Travis Hardin. Travis, my sister Marie."

Travis nodded. "Pleasure, Marie."

"Pleased to meet…" She looked directly at Travis. "Has anyone ever told you that you have a very strong aura?"

Travis looked at Shelby, then back at Marie. "No. Don't believe they have."

"Uh, Marie, Travis is from Texas. He's looking at a couple of mares from the farm."

When Travis stepped to Shelby's side, Marie's eyes

widened. "Excuse us a moment, will you?" She pulled her sister toward the back of the shop.

"What?" Shelby said.

"It's you and Travis," Marie whispered.

"What about us?"

"Well, it's your auras. They're…"

"They're what?"

"Dynamite. The instant you were close enough to touch, both of your auras went from green to warm blue so fast it took my breath away."

Shelby glanced at Travis, who was trying to look interested in some voodoo items. "Refresh my memory. Is that good or bad?"

"It's fantastic! I've never seen so much passion and power between two people."

Shelby cut Travis another look and smiled. "Really."

"If the two of you ever make love it will be…well, very…"

"Are you trying to tell me the earth will move?"

"That's a distinct possibility."

From the look in Marie's eyes, Shelby realized she was dead serious. "Really?"

"No doubt about it. If you're not interested, I can give you some camphor oil. It has some properties that will cool—"

"That won't be necessary."

Marie smiled. "No camphor, huh?"

Smiling, Shelby shook her head as they rejoined Travis, who was reading labels.

"Do people really think this stuff works?" he asked Marie.

"Some do, but it's mostly for tourists. My ultimate goal is to get rid of this and concentrate on aromatherapy. However, for the time being, voodoo trappings are more reliable for paying the rent than oils and candles. That reminds me,'' she said to Shelby. ''Come into the back. I'm mixing up something for you to take to Aunt Mary.''

Through the curtain of beads was another room with shelves completely covering two adjoining walls, while the other two walls were draped in a heavy fabric. There was no natural light in the room, only illumination from candles. Lots of candles. In one corner was a worktable containing an assortment of bottles and jars.

Marie walked to the table, opened the top drawer of an apothecary chest and removed a tiny envelope. She then sprinkled some of the contents into a bottle of oil. ''I've also got a black glass amulet I want you to give to her, as well,'' she said carefully, mixing powder and oil. ''It's that one.'' She pointed to a pendant lying on the worktable, but never broke her focus on preparing the oil. Her concentration was so complete she seemed unaware Shelby had walked up and was standing beside her.

Shelby leaned over the amulet for a closer look. The setting for the teardrop stone was a delicate silver filigree. ''Unique setting,'' she commented, admiring the stone. ''You're so sweet to do this for Aunt Mary. I know she'll appreciate it.''

As Shelby raised her head, Marie turned, the open bottle in her hand, and they collided.

Travis saw what was about to happen, but he didn't get the warning out fast enough. ''Hey,'' he called just as the collision jarred the bottle in Marie's hand, slinging most of the contents all down the left side of

Shelby's head. Both women squealed and jumped back, but the damage was already done.

"Oh, Shelby, I'm so sorry." Instantly, Marie set the bottle down and yanked a towel from a nearby rack. Quickly, she dabbed at the spot, but the oil had already seeped into Shelby's hair, leaving one side limp and stringy. "I didn't realize you were so close."

"It's not your fault. I wasn't paying attention, either. Besides, it was an accident."

"But your hair," Marie wailed.

"Oh, yeah." Shelby touched the limp strands. "Can't go strolling along the Riverwalk like this, can I? Well, I'll just go upstairs and shampoo my hair. You don't mind, do you, Travis? It won't take—"

"I'm out of shampoo."

"Out? But you mix your own."

"I used the last of it this morning, and I've been so busy I haven't had time to mix more. I was going to do it tonight after the Wicca lecture I'm supposed to attend..." Marie cast an apologetic glance at Travis. "I really am sorry. I know this puts a crimp in your plans."

He just shook his head. Of course he could never say so, but the whole situation was more comical than tragic. Marie trying to wipe oil out of her sister's hair, and Shelby looking like the "before" in a shampoo commercial.

"Don't be silly," Shelby said. "There's bound to be a convenience store not far from here. I'll buy some shampoo and be back in no time."

"Not within walking distance. They've got the sidewalk torn up in front of the one right around the corner in order to repair the street. The owner has

been screaming bloody murder to the city, but..."
Marie shrugged.

"This doesn't seem to be my day." Shelby thought
for a minute, then looked at Travis. "Well, I'm not
going to let this spoil everything, so I'll drive to a
store if I have to."

"Didn't you say you parked on Dumaine?" Marie
asked.

"Yes."

"If you head north to Rampart and turn right,
there's a drugstore about a half a block down. But—"
Marie pointed to the limp hair "—you can't go like
that. I'll be right back." She grabbed a handful of
drapery, jerked it aside and opened a door that Travis
hadn't even realized was there. She stepped through
the door and seconds later returned holding several
colorful scarves.

"Here." She held one with bright flowers out to
Shelby, then changed her mind.

"Try the purple one. It's very soothing."

"Marie—"

"No, here's the one." She tossed the others away,
and they floated gracefully to the floor. "Somebody
gave it to me." She frowned in earnest.

"I did. Last Christmas."

"No wonder I thought it looked like you."

Shelby sighed, then glanced at Travis. He was
standing there watching, trying not to laugh. "Don't
you dare so much as crack a smile, Travis Hardin."

"Who, me?" But he turned his head so she
wouldn't see his grin. "Just waiting on you, darlin'."

"Better take your jacket off," Marie advised.
"There's a spot of oil on the shoulder."

"Great," Shelby said, slipping out of her jacket,

which Travis gallantly stepped forward and took from her. "Thanks."

"Want me to tie the scarf for you?" Marie touched her own. "I've had lots of practice."

"No, thank you." Shelby turned and walked back into the front of the shop to stand before an antique mirror hanging on the wall next to a rack of Mardi Gras masks. She pushed her dark hair back, positioned the scarf and tied it at the back of her neck in a peasant fashion.

"You should add scarves to your wardrobe, Shelby. I mean it. You look great."

Shelby looked at her sister's sweet face and didn't have the heart to scold her. But then, no one ever did. "Scarves are *your* trademark." She leaned over and gave her a hug. "I think one trademark per family is enough."

Marie shrugged. "Suit yourself."

Shelby looked at Travis. "I appreciate the fact that you've kept your smirking under control during this…debacle."

"Most fun I've had in I can't tell you when, darlin'."

"So glad to be able to amuse you. C'mon, let's get out of here before something else happens." She turned to Marie. "We'll be right back."

"Bye."

Outside on the street, Shelby glanced up at Travis. "You should be ashamed of yourself."

"What for?"

"Enjoying the misfortune of others."

He grinned. "Misfortune, huh? Looked like a downright mess to me."

"That's exactly what I look like—a mess. Thanks for reminding me."

She elbowed him in the ribs just as a man hurried out of a shop and brushed past her, almost knocking her into Travis. He was quick to take advantage of the situation, slipping his arm around her waist.

"Darlin'," he said, gazing into her eyes, "if you're a mess, then you're the sexiest mess I've ever seen."

She put her hand on his shoulder to steady herself, hoping no one else on the street could see her sudden agitation. "Sexy?" Maybe Marie was right on target.

"Absolutely." With one hand still firmly around her waist, he reached up with his other one and flicked the tiny gold hoop dangling from her right earlobe. "You look like a wild gypsy princess."

"Wild, huh?"

"Definitely," he whispered as he touched his mouth to hers.

Somewhere in the back of her mind Shelby knew they were standing on a busy street in the French Quarter in broad daylight with people staring at them. But her body didn't care. Maybe it was shameless, or maybe it was giving free rein to the feelings he inspired. Either way, she loved it.

Travis drew back just enough to rub his mouth over hers. Slowly.

"Hmm." She sighed against his lips and felt him smile.

"If I don't stop kissing you now, we'll be in big trouble."

"Too late. I was in big trouble the minute I met you."

"Can we get arrested for doing this?"

"Not if we stop now."

They looked at each other and grinned.

"Okay." Travis slipped his arm from her waist to hold her hand. "Let's find your little red convertible and cool off."

As they approached the car, he headed for the passenger side and Shelby stepped into the street, fishing in her purse for her keys. The top was down, so Travis reached for the door. "Some of Marie's oil spilled into your purse and the keys keep slipping out of your fingers?"

"Very funny."

"Yeah, well—"

Before he could say another word, a car came barreling down the street behind Shelby. Oblivious to any danger, she looked up with a wide smile, clutching her purse to her chest with one hand and waving the keys with the other. "Got 'em."

"Shelby!"

She heard the sudden terror in Travis's voice and the roar of the car's engine almost simultaneously. The next instant she felt air whoosh past her body and something slam into her arm. The car keys flew out of her hand, then everything started to spin.

Horrified, Travis watched as the speeding car's side mirror caught Shelby, spinning her around, then rolling her forward along the side of the convertible. His heart almost stopped when he heard her scream. He tried to run around the car, tried to get to her, but his feet seemed to be encased in cement. What took no more than a few seconds unfolded like horrifying hours of slow-motion footage. Then the edge of the windshield stopped her momentum. As the car sped past, Shelby pitched forward into the convertible, her head grazing the steering wheel.

Travis dashed around to the driver's side, yanked open the door and reached to pick her up. The instant he touched her she moaned.

"Oh, God," he said, trying to see how badly she was hurt without hurting her himself. "Shelby. Darlin', talk to me. Shelby, are you all right?"

"T-Travis," she managed to whisper.

"That's it, darlin'. Talk to me. Did you hit your head? Tell me where you're hurt."

Slowly she sat up. "Travis?"

"Right here, darlin'. Right here."

Her eyes focused on his face. "Hurt?" For a second she was disoriented. "What...what happened?"

"Some sonuvabitch—" he gritted his teeth and she realized he was trembling "—almost ran you down."

"He hit me?"

"For a second I thought..." The image of that reality was too horrendous to think about. Travis shook his head. "No. Not the car. Caught you with the side mirror."

"He didn't see me?"

"Obviously—"

"Why didn't he stop?"

"Dammit, Shelby. Stop asking questions and answer one. Did you hit your head?"

She touched her right temple and forehead, shoving the scarf off her head. "N-no. I just sort of slid over the steering wheel. I think."

"You think? That's not good enough. I'm taking you to the emergency room."

"No. I—I don't think I need to." She looked up at him, her eyes now clear and focused. "Really."

With infinite tenderness he put his hand on her cheek, then gently threaded his fingers through her hair to check for cuts or bumps. There were none. Relief flowed through him. "What about your chest? You hit the edge of the windshield."

Shelby glanced down and discovered she was still clutching her purse to her chest. An indentation in the handbag divided it almost perfectly in half, leaving a rip in the leather. She looked up at Travis, and comprehension struck like the car that hadn't.

Her eyes now wide with shock, Shelby experienced everything once more in a blinding flash. Travis screaming her name. The impact of something hitting her from behind. The sensation that the world was spinning off its axis. She could have been seriously hurt. She could have been killed. But the most sobering awareness was not just that her life could have ended. It was the realization that she would never have had the chance to love Travis.

No. That wasn't true.

She already loved him.

Dear Lord, what a liar she had been. She'd told him that she didn't smell orange blossoms when she kissed him, and it was one big fat lie. She wanted it all—orange blossoms, kids, a lifetime of loving him...

"Shelby? Talk to me, darlin'—"

"I—I..." She glanced down at the damaged purse, then back at him. "Travis," she whispered, her eyes filling with tears as she reached for him.

He wrapped his arms around her, held her as tightly as he dared for fear of hurting her further. "It's all right, darlin'. You're safe. It's okay." As much as he hated releasing her, he was compelled to make sure she truly was all right. "I still think you should see a doctor. Just to be sure nothing is broken."

Shelby shook her head and was relieved not to hear anything rattle. As for her stunning insight a second ago, she had a feeling that would be much more traumatizing than her near miss with a demented driver. "Will you take me back to Marie's shop?" she murmured. She needed to think, to put everything into perspective.

"What? No, I'm taking you to a hospital."

"That's really not necessary."

Travis didn't know if she was still dazed or just needed the comfort of her sister. Either way, he didn't like it. He wouldn't be satisfied until he heard a doctor pronounce her healthy. "Shelby—"

"Please, Travis. Take me to Marie's."

He hesitated but finally gave in. "All right, but five minutes, then we're on our way to the emergency room." He helped her out of the car, and she swayed against him. Immediately he wrapped his arms around her. "Please, let me—"

"I'm fine. Really." She straightened, took several deep breaths and was steady on her feet. The need to lean against him was so strong it was frightening. She wanted to fling herself back into his arms and tell him how much she loved him. How much she needed him. But she had done that to a man once before and it had cost her dearly. At the moment her emotions were too fragile. She had to pull herself together before she could deal with what all of this would mean.

"I really am okay, Travis. But that doesn't mean I wouldn't enjoy having your arm around me while we walk back."

He stared at her, wondering if she was as fine as she claimed or if she was being brave on his account.

So help him, if she was being brave he was going to strangle her. "Sure this is what you want?"

"Positive."

"I'm doing this under protest," he insisted, helping her down the street toward Marie's shop.

"So noted."

"Don't get cute, counselor. I just got the hell scared out of me, and I'm in no mood to play fair."

She smiled up at him. "Overruled."

They were three doors away from Heaven Scent when Shelby leaned her head on Travis's shoulder. He took the gesture as a sign that she felt weak and scooped her up into his arms.

"What are you doing?"

"Carrying you."

"Why?"

"I thought you were about to faint."

"Why would you think that?"

"Because you laid… Never mind. Just be quiet and enjoy the ride."

Truthfully, she did. There was definitely something to be said for being carried around in the arms of a handsome man. Her handsome man. The man she loved.

When they came through the door to the shop, Marie looked up from the cash register, where she was tallying a customer's purchases. "Good heavens. What happened?"

"Close call with an idiot driver."

"Oh, Shelby, honey! Take her to my apartment. I'll be right up."

Travis stepped through the curtain of beads, glancing around.

"You can put me down now." As soon as her feet

touched the floor, Shelby crossed the room and grabbed a handful of drapery, pulling it back to expose a door. She opened it and started up a narrow flight of stairs.

"Wait!" Travis hurried after her, helping her from behind until they reached the large, airy loft at the top of the stairs. As with his first impression of Heaven Scent, a heady fragrance dominated the air—this one something he couldn't quite identify.

Shelby headed for a small kitchenette with a table and two chairs tucked into a corner of the room. "I need a drink of water. Want one?" she asked.

"Not unless it's got at least two shots of bourbon mixed with it."

"Marie doesn't drink."

"Figures," he mumbled.

He was about to ask directions to the nearest liquor store when Marie showed up carrying a bottle similar to the one she'd been holding when she and Shelby collided earlier.

"I've mixed some jojoba oil with juniper and some eucalyptus. It should do the trick."

"What trick?" Travis asked.

"Immediate healing, of course," Marie said.

"Excuse me?"

Shelby walked to where they stood. "I told you, Marie is a herbalist. Her lotions and oils have amazing restorative powers."

"You mean to tell me—"

"Let me have a look at you," Marie said. "Are you dizzy, nauseous or seeing lights?"

"No."

"Your pupils aren't dilated. What about all your joints?" Gently, Marie tested them in the same manner Travis had. "Everything seems to be in working order."

"I have to admit my knees are a little weak, but I think that's just the terror and adrenaline wearing off."

"Probably," Marie agreed. "You're going to have a nasty bruise on the back of your arm."

Shelby glanced over her shoulder. "Yeah, a real whopper."

"Will the two of you stop talking as if she just broke a fingernail?" Travis demanded.

Both women looked at him. "He's very upset—" Shelby began.

"Damn straight."

"He saw the car coming and tried to save me."

Travis ran his hands through his hair. "But I couldn't get there."

Shelby stepped close to him. "Travis, you're not Superman. I didn't expect you to fly over the car and whisk me away to safety."

The urge to touch her was so powerful he trembled with it. He reached out a hand, hesitated, then stroked her cheek with the back of his fingers. "I think my heart stopped beating when I heard you scream. I was…" He swallowed hard. "If anything had happened to you—"

"It didn't and I'm fine. But I'd be better if you held me." She sighed as he gathered her in his arms. "Much better."

Watching the interchange, Marie smiled. "I need to get downstairs and close up." She set the bottle on the table and slipped out of the room. Neither Shelby or Travis noticed that she left.

"You should be sitting down," he said, holding her closer.

"I like where I am."

"God, you're hardheaded." With that he picked her up and carried her to one of the two chaise longues in the room. At least he thought they were chaise longues, but he wasn't sure, since they weren't upholstered, but draped in fabric. The only other furniture in the room was a king-size bed, so he took a chance on the supposed chaise.

"I prefer to think of it as determined," she informed him as he slipped off her shoes.

"I'll bet you do. You want a blanket or something?" He had never felt so totally useless in his whole life. "Why don't you let me call Marie's doctor, and at least—"

"Marie *is* her doctor."

"Listen, darlin'. Nothing against your sister, but—"

"There you are." Marie materialized from the stairwell and came toward them. "I see you're taking excellent care of her, Travis." She struck a long match and lit two candles sitting on a low table between the chaise longues.

"I'd feel better if she would see a doctor," he mumbled.

"Of course you would." Holding the match, she walked to the nightstand beside the bed and lit another candle, then another and another, finally blowing out the match. "Most people find it difficult to trust something they don't understand. But this will do wonders." She picked up the oil concoction. "I promise."

Travis looked askance at the container. "Is she supposed to drink it?"

"Of course not. You're supposed to rub it into the skin." She pointed at Travis. "And I do mean you. Shelby needs a long, hot shower, then you must rub the oil all over her body. Well, you don't have to cover the soles of her feet," she amended. "But certainly any spot that might be bruised or tender."

"But won't that hurt like hell?"

"A little, but the oil will help it hurt a lot less when she wakes up tomorrow." When Travis gave her a dubious look, Marie placed the bottle in his hands. "Travis, I love Shelby. She's very dear to me, and I would never do anything that might cause her harm. Please believe me when I tell you that she has no broken bones, no lasting damage. I'm not some kind of cultist or crackpot. If I thought she needed a doctor we wouldn't be standing here, we'd be on our way to the ER."

Maybe it was the conviction in her voice or the way it softened when she spoke Shelby's name, but Travis believed her. And Shelby trusted her.

"All right."

"Thank you, Travis," Marie said, then turned to Shelby. "Can I get anything else for you?"

"No. I thought you had a lecture tonight."

"I do, but I'll cancel if you'd feel better with me here."

"Heavens, no. Please go, enjoy yourself."

"All right. I won't be back until—" she gave her sister a knowing look "—very late. Make yourselves at home." With a smile and a wave, Marie disappeared back down the stairwell. A few seconds later they heard the bell over the shop door jingle as it closed.

When Travis shook his head, Shelby laughed. "I told you she sees life from a different perspective."

"Yeah. I just didn't know how different."

"If it will keep you from fretting, I promise that if I feel worse within an hour, I'll let you take me to see a doctor. How's that?"

"Acceptable...barely."

She swung her legs over the edge of the chaise, took the oil from him and set it next to the candles. "I think I'll have that shower Marie recommended. Between my oily hairdo and my encounter with a rogue side mirror, I could use it."

"No shampoo, remember." When she turned with a pleading look in her eyes, he held up his hand. "Don't even think about it. You couldn't get me away from here with a stick of dynamite."

"But Travis—"

"Use bar soap."

"Ugh."

"I mean it, Shelby. I'm not going anywhere until I make sure you're all right."

Bar soap would have to do, she decided. Besides, she had more important things to consider. Like the fact that she had just discovered she was totally, completely in love with him. She smiled, then walked into the bathroom. Once inside, she closed the door and sagged against it.

The thought shocked her and thrilled her all at the same time. She wasn't sure when exactly she had fallen so desperately in love with him, but she suspected it might very well have been the first moment she saw him. Remembering her immediate and powerful reaction to him, she didn't doubt it. The bizarre thing was that she had always said she didn't believe in love at first sight. It wasn't possible. Lust at first sight, yes, but not love. She pushed away from the door and looked in the mirror.

"Now what?" she asked her reflection.

She wasn't completely certain how to handle this new development. Her track record being what it was, she definitely didn't want to make a wrong move. She had never been one to throw caution to the wind, but with Travis, she hadn't felt as if there had been any wrong moves. Everything about their relationship from the first second had felt right. She hadn't questioned whether or not he was sincere, because she trusted him. Nothing about her time with Travis resembled her time with Royce, and she realized it was because she had learned to trust herself, her instincts. Her instincts had assured her he was trustworthy, and they hadn't let her down. This time she was in love with the right man.

Even if he didn't love her?

Shelby thought about that as she turned on the shower, then stepped beneath the warm, stinging spray. He wanted her, and several times she had sensed that he was ready for more than just a casual affair, yet he held back. Maybe he had some demons lurking in his own past. And maybe he wouldn't be able to overcome them enough to love her. Shelby only knew that she wasn't willing to stifle her feelings anymore. If she had learned nothing else from her episode with Royce, she had learned that she had a right to them.

One thing she had told Travis was true—if he left, she would be hurt, but she would survive. Without knowing it, he had given her a precious gift—the gift of loving. If they couldn't share that gift, she would be heartbroken. And still grateful.

The only way to handle the situation, she decided as she finished her shower, was the only way she knew how. Honestly.

# CHAPTER TEN

AS WITH SHELBY, the effects of the near miss had taken a toll on Travis. He still couldn't believe she was in one piece. Every time he thought about how close she had come to being seriously hurt, his gut tightened. If he lived to be a hundred he would never forget the instant he'd looked up and seen the car roaring along the street. It had seemed to come out of nowhere. One minute is wasn't there, the next it was barreling down on Shelby as if deliberately aiming for her. Everything happened so fast he didn't remember much about the car except that it was tan, or maybe gold, and big. Possibly a 1970 Buick or Plymouth. Not that any of what he remembered made any difference without the license number.

His hands curled into fists as he thought about getting hold of the careless driver. *Relax,* he told himself. Shelby seemed to be okay, and spending the night in jail for busting some unknown, and probably drunk, driver in the jaw wouldn't do anyone any good.

He heard the shower stop, and a few seconds later the sound of a hair dryer. Restless, he walked to the bank of windows facing St. Ann Street and gazed out as dusk dissolved into evening. Behind him he heard the hair dryer stop and the bathroom door open.

"Whenever you feel up to it," he said, turning around, "we can…"

The rest of the sentence died on his lips, the rest of his thoughts right along with it. All he could do was stare as Shelby came toward him wearing nothing but a towel.

"Ready?" she asked.

"What?"

"Are you ready to rub the oil on me?"

"Uh…" He could have jumped out the window with more sangfroid than doing that. "I guess so."

"Would you mind closing the shutters?" she asked as she walked over to the table, picked up the container of oil, then moved to the bed and sat down. She looked at him over her shoulder. "Travis?"

"Yeah. Sure." He closed the shutters, leaving the room illuminated only by the glow of the half dozen or so candles Marie had lit. Then he came to stand beside her. She handed him the oil, then lifted the mass of dark hair off her neck, presenting him with her back.

As if his pulse wasn't hammering enough, it went into double time when she loosened the knot over her breasts and the towel slipped, exposing her smooth back almost to her waist. Travis wet his suddenly dry lips and tried to concentrate on the fact that he would be touching her smooth skin for strictly medicinal purposes.

Yeah, right.

Carefully, he poured a few drops of oil into the palm of his right hand, then began to spread it on her shoulders. She moaned.

"I'm hurting you—"

"No. It feels good."

Cautiously, he started massaging her shoulder again. "Let me know if I hit a sore spot." To his surprise, the oil didn't stay on top of her skin, but seemed to penetrate quickly, leaving her soft skin even softer.

"Hmm." She sighed, knowing exactly the effect she was having on him. Knowing she was taking a big risk. She was laying it all on the line for him. Her body, her heart. He just needed a nudge, and if this didn't do, nothing would. "Why don't you put the container on the table next to you? Then you can use both hands."

Both hands. Great, just what he needed. Why didn't he just cut his throat and be done with it?

"Oh, that feels wonderful." She lifted her left arm, the one rapidly showing signs of a huge bruise. "Might want to put a little extra here."

He took her hand, got more oil and started rubbing. Up her arm, across her shoulders and down the other arm. All the way down her back to her hips and up again. Her neck, the top of her shoulders, her collarbone. Almost to the swell of her breast...

"Hmm." Closing her eyes, she let her head loll back, giving him greater access.

"Shelby."

"Yes."

"I have to stop."

She opened her eyes and noticed that his hands were shaking. "Why? We—"

"Because if I don't, things are going to get real hot, real quick."

"But—"

"Give me a break, darlin'. I'm trying to be a gentleman, but it's getting tougher by the minute."

Holding the towel deliciously low over her breasts, Shelby stood up and faced him. "Then, stop trying."

"Shelby." To his credit, he actually took a step back. "I don't think—"

"No, Travis, that's your problem. You think too much. You think you can avoid what's happening between us, but you can't. You might even think I'm too upset to make love. Wrong. If I needed a reminder of how short life can be, I got it today." She stepped so close to him she had to look up in order to see his face. As she had the first time they kissed, she took the initiative. "I want you to kiss me. Make love with me."

"Shelby, that's not a good idea—"

"Don't you want me?"

"Are you crazy?"

"No."

"Then, you know the answer to that one."

"So what's the problem?"

If she only knew. He was tempted to tell her, to spill his guts right here, right now. That way she could hate him and he could justify his guilt. "I just don't think that—"

"There you go again. Thinking." Still clutching the towel, she ran her other hand over his chest.

"One of us has to."

His need for her was a relentless, slow-burning fire in his gut, one that was getting hotter by the second. He was dizzy with the urge to feel her oiled, satiny skin against his body, but he kept his hands at his sides, knowing one more touch was all it would take for him to lose control.

"No, we need to feel." She rose up on her toes and skimmed the tip of her tongue over his bottom lip. "Travis…"

The fire in his gut exploded fueled by raw, urgent

desire. He lost it. Yet even as his hands grasped her shoulders, he tried to temper the need to throw her on the bed and take her quickly. Even as his mouth crushed hers he tried to hang on to enough of his sanity not to ravish her.

He couldn't get enough of her. No matter how close he held her, no matter how he devoured her mouth, it wasn't enough. In his blinding need for more he pulled her down onto the bed, rolling her beneath him.

She had been about to tell him her feelings, but his kiss was so quick and demanding she barely had time to draw a breath.

"Travis," she whispered when he finally pulled his mouth from hers, "please...I need—"

"I need you, too. God, how I need you."

He lifted his leg across her body, much the same way she had done to him the day before. Only this time she wasn't in control—he was. This time she couldn't get away. For a moment, old fears nipped at her and she reacted instinctively, struggling against him.

It took him a second to realize her movements were resistance, not passion. Thinking he had touched a bruise, he drew back instantly. "I'm sorry, darlin'. Did I hurt you?"

"No," she said, but there were tears in her eyes.

A couple of seconds ticked by before it dawned on him what she might be concerned about. "If you're worried about protection—"

"No. That's not... Travis, I need to tell you something first." She moved away from him, to the edge of the bed. "I should have said something before I kissed you... I—"

"You sure I didn't hurt you? My hands are rough and—"

"I'm sure." She gathered the towel closer. "But I need to tell you something."

He reached over and covered her hand with his. "All right."

"My last year in law school, I was…I had a relationship with another student. I thought I was in love—no," she corrected herself. "I was in love with him, and I thought he was in love with me. My family liked him. Granddad even hinted there might be a place for him in the firm. One night we were at his apartment. In bed. We started playing silly games." She gripped the towel tighter. "You know, tickling each other, playful nudges, that kind of stuff. Then he threw me down on the bed and refused to let me up. At first I was just pretending to struggle, but he kept holding me down, tighter and tighter. When I told him I didn't want to go any further, he still wouldn't let me up. He was really aroused. And the more I struggled, the more excited he became."

She took a deep breath, licking her lips, and Travis knew he wasn't going to like what he was about to hear. He also knew he had to hear it.

"I panicked. Started to scream, bite, scratch. Anything to make him let me go. But I just made it worse. Something snapped and he went a little crazy. He—" she closed her eyes "—he raped me."

Travis fought an overwhelming urge to pull her into his arms, gather her close, but he didn't think that was what she needed at the moment.

Slowly, she opened her eyes, but she didn't look at him. "When it was over he cried, begged my forgiveness, pledged his everlasting devotion. Even asked me to marry him.''

If the rape hadn't been enough for Travis to want the man dead, the proposal cinched it. To a woman like Shelby, that must have been the final insult.

''As if that wasn't enough of an insult,'' she said, voicing his thought, ''the next day he sent me a dozen long-stemmed roses with a mushy note, and called an hour later still vowing his love. And I started to weaken.'' She looked at Travis. ''Right up until he asked if I had told Granddad what happened. Not had I called the dean, or even the police. His only real concern was his standing with Delacroix and Associates. I hung up on him, and haven't seen or spoken to him since.''

''Darlin', I'm so sorry. I'm sorry you went though something so awful, and I'm sorry I made it worse.''

''You didn't.''

''You asked me why I didn't press my advantage the first time we kissed. And you told me no one had turned you on in a long time. How dense could I be? Hell, you might as well have plastered a sign on your chest reading Fragile—Handle With Care.''

''Travis…'' She put her hand in his. ''You didn't make it worse. Therapy helped me see that not only was I not at fault, I couldn't have prevented it. If anything, you've helped me. Falling in love with you has…''

At his stunned expression, she said, ''I could have said that better. You probably think I lied to you. Because I do smell orange blossoms when I kiss you, Travis,'' Shelby admitted in a rush. ''And think about commitment. That's why I needed to tell you about the rape. You've given me back passion and joy. If I didn't love you for any other reason, I would love you for that. But the truth is, my heart and soul belong to you. And," she said, catching a breath, "I've probably scared you to death, but I had to be honest about my feelings."

When he still didn't respond, she added, "By the way, my declaration makes no demands on you." She got up from the bed and started toward the bathroom. "You know, one of these days I'm going to learn how to tell the truth without being so blunt. They don't call it being brutally honest for nothing. I'm sorry—"

"Shelby."

She stopped, turned to face him. And waited. Hoped.

Travis walked over to her, reached out to touch her, then drew his hand back. "Don't apologize. Not ever, and especially not to me. And don't ever change."

"You're not going to head for the hills?"

"Not likely."

"I won't take that as a commitment."

The truth was he wanted her to take it as just that. Only he couldn't very well make such an offer without being as honest as she had. "Shelby, I need to tell you—"

"No. I didn't tell you I love you just so I could hear you repeat the words to me. I don't want you to say anything right now. I only discovered I was in love with you an hour ago, so in a way, this is as new to me as it is to you. Tonight I want to make love and enjoy all these delicious feelings. Whatever you have to say, please let it wait until tomorrow."

He knew he should demand that she listen. He knew he should tell her the truth whether she wanted to hear it or not. But he wanted this time with her—

a few short, sweet hours that he could remember when she was gone from him. Call it cowardice. Call it greed. Call it a desperate grasp for something too fine and rare to ever really be his. But this was his only chance, and Travis knew it. He would undoubtedly burn in hell for what he was about to do, but right or wrong, good or bad, he needed her. He had needed her all his life.

He slipped his hand to the back of her neck. This time when his mouth touched hers there was no crush, no rush. Instead, angling his mouth against hers, using his tongue with gentle force, he commanded her lips to part. When they did, he savored every luscious second, drawing the kiss out, wanting to make everything soft and wonderful for her. She deserved sweetness.

"Travis, Travis," she murmured against his lips. "I'm not a china doll and—"

"Yeah, you are."

"I don't need you to treat me like one."

"You're delicate—"

"And you're not listening. I just said you gave me back passion and joy. That's what I want. Please." She nuzzled closer. "Don't make me beg."

He was a lot of things, but a saint wasn't one of them. This time when she pressed closer still, he didn't back away. "I should be the one begging," he said a second before his mouth claimed hers yet again.

Shelby gave herself over to the kiss, letting it sweep her up in the promise of passion. This was what she wanted, needed. Arching her back, she pressed her body to his, loving the feel of his hard-muscled strength. She offered no resistance when he tugged the towel from her body, flung it aside and scooped her up in his arms. He carried her the few remaining steps to the bed, pulled back the white eyelet coverlet and lowered her onto the sheet.

"So perfect," he said, gazing at her sleek body, her skin like ivory satin in the candlelight.

For a heartbeat she fought the urge to cover herself. Then she remembered that this was Travis. The past was gone, and he was her here and now. Maybe even her future. She relaxed and let him look his fill. He ran his hands from her collarbone to her knees, then back again, leaving a sizzling trail of sensations. She reached for him, wanting to touch him the way he was touching her.

"No fair." She began unbuttoning his shirt. "I want to feel all of you next to all of me."

"You have any idea what it does to me to hear you say things like that?"

"Same thing it does to me, I hope."

For the first time since he had turned and found her wearing nothing but the towel, he smiled. "Makes me crazy. How about you?"

"Hmm." She freed the last button, pushed the shirt down over his shoulders. "Makes me crazy for you, period. There…" She sighed, running her hands over his bare chest. "Oh, yes."

As he lowered his mouth for another ravenous kiss, her breasts touched his chest and Travis groaned. Instinctively, Shelby raised her leg over his, eager to be closer. Everything about him was hard and wild—his hands, his mouth, his body—and she loved it. She felt the taut muscles of his shoulder and back as she ran her palm over his skin, needing him closer.

"I'm too heavy," he insisted.

"No. No. I can't touch you enough, get close enough. Please," she said, tugging at his jeans. She got his complete cooperation, and in moments they were in the bed, naked.

Oh, his mouth. It was hot, greedy and everywhere. With every touch, every stroke, he obliterated that night three years earlier, wiped it away forever. She realized that until now she hadn't really known what passion was. Not real passion. Not this mindless craving. And the more he gave, the more she wanted.

He murmured her name as he feasted on her soft breasts and the tender flesh just below her navel. His tongue did wicked, wonderful things, and she moved restlessly, yearning. She was on fire, burning from the inside out, yet she wanted more. She rocked against him and heard his breath hiss between his teeth. A part of her rejoiced that she could weaken his control as he had hers.

But she didn't know what fire was until his hand cupped her, his fingers stroking, driving her toward a madness she craved. She called his name once, then, her body taut with need, shuddered as he drove her over the edge.

He felt her body contract and explode, and it was all he could do to stay in control. But he wanted her to experience the full measure of passion.

"Travis," she said with a ragged sigh, even as he drove her higher once again. "Please…"

Then her fingers closed around him, and he knew he couldn't stand another second of not being inside her. He plunged deep, all rational thought obliterated. There was only Shelby, and the sweet, dark tide of desire they created together.

THE RINGING OF THE PHONE woke them. Without opening her eyes, Shelby patted her hand over the pillow and across the bedside table until she reached the phone. Eyes still closed, she put the receiver to her ear. "Hello. Oh, yes. Sorry. Oh, good," she said, and hung up.

Travis, propped up on one elbow, looked down at her. "Are you awake enough to carry on a conversation?"

"Hmm."

He grinned. "My point exactly." He ran a hand over her bare back down to her waist. "Shelby."

"Hmm."

"You know Marie would probably appreciate it if we weren't in her bed when she gets home."

Shelby turned her head and opened one eye. "That was her on the phone."

"Asking us to leave?"

Now she propped herself up on her elbow, facing him. "She's staying the night with a friend, so we've got a choice. We could get dressed and drive back to Bayou Beltane, or we could—"

He pulled her into his arms. "No contest, darlin'."

"I want you again," she said, kissing his neck.

"Now we've got time to take it slow and easy." The last thing he wanted was slow and easy, but he was determined to savor her, treasure her, show her how much he cared.

"Hmm. We could do that."

"We should," he said, his breathing growing harder by the minute, not to mention a certain part of his anatomy.

Shelby pushed him onto his back and straddled his hips. She moved, rocking harder and harder, reveling in being control. Power, sweet and heady, surged through her. She moaned as he cupped her breasts in his hands, then threw her head back in pure ecstasy when he replaced them with his mouth.

"Next time slow and easy," she whispered, as pleasure jolted through her. Pressure built inside her until, wild with need, she exploded once more in a blaze of white heat.

Before she could recover, he had reversed their positions and plunged into her. With each thrust he drove deeper, harder, and she rose to meet him— equals in passion, until they were equally spent.

## CHAPTER ELEVEN

TRAVIS HAD TO ADMIT that watching dawn break, speeding along the Twin Span crossing Lake Pontchartrain, his arm around Shelby, was a terrific way to start any day. When they turned into the driveway at Riverwood, he hated the idea of being without her.

"Guess I better go in," she said with a yawn.

"Before your grandfather comes out with a shotgun?"

"Don't be silly. He owns dueling pistols."

"Oh, great. Makes me feel much better."

Shelby looped her arms around Travis's neck, and danced a line of kisses from his ear to his mouth. "You feel wonderful." She kissed him deeply. "You taste pretty good, too."

The sun was almost up. Soon the household would be stirring, if it wasn't already. Travis needed to let her go, but he didn't want to. In fact, he'd like nothing better than to turn the car around, drive straight to his motel and make love to her all day long.

"I hate to say goodbye."

"Yeah." He brushed a strand of hair from her cheek.

"You know, after laying my cards on the table, so to speak, I guess you wouldn't think I was too forward if I asked when I'll see you again."

Travis nuzzled her cheek and chuckled. "Not forward—honest. It's one of the things I...admire most about you.'' Had he almost said "love?" God, things were getting more complicated by the hour.

"Well, I can honestly say that last night was one of the best, if not *the* best night of my life. And in the light of a new day, I have no regrets. I take nothing back.''

He knew she was referring to the fact that she had told him she loved him. That much honesty was harder to deal with than he had expected. But it was one of the things he admired most about her. One of the many things. After last night he realized just how totally unique she was. Rare and fine. What his grandmother would have called a sweet treasure.

"Do you know how special you are?'' he asked, holding her delicate face between his hands. "You make me feel things I never expected to feel. You strolled into my life, and I don't think it will ever be the same. What am I going to do with you?''

*Love me,* she wanted to say but didn't dare. She had meant every word she'd said last night. There was no going back. No changing directions. She loved him, and in her heart she was almost certain he loved her. While she clung to that hope, she wouldn't crowd him.

"Don't you know better than to ask a lawyer such a loaded question?'' She kissed him again, letting her greedy lips, and her body pressed close to his, answer for her.

"I think I hear your granddaddy loading those pistols. One more kiss and then I'm outta here,'' he said, without conviction.

It turned out to be several more kisses before either of them could actually regain enough reason to stop.

"Seriously, darlin', you being gone all night isn't going to cause problems, is it?"

"No. I'm sure Granddad would prefer the good old days when young women didn't dare go against rules and traditions, but I have an advantage. Except for Joanna, I'm the first Delacroix to join the family business in more than twenty years. He and Dad are so thrilled, I can almost get away with murder. So," she said, kissing Travis again, "while they may not like it, they respect my right to live my own life, and I respect them enough not to go wild."

"You don't have the wild-child look about you."

"Actually, this is my first walk on the wild side." She grinned. "I like it."

"Think I've got myself a dangerous woman."

"Count on it, cowboy." And she gave him one final kiss, hot enough to keep him warm all day.

As Travis watched her walk up the steps and into the house, he prayed that when the crunch came she would love him enough to understand. For a woman like Shelby, lying was a cardinal sin. As he walked toward his truck, he just hoped it wasn't an unforgivable one.

HIS PHONE WAS RINGING when he opened his motel-room door.

"Where the hell have you been?" T.C. demanded as soon as Travis answered.

"Sorry, Dad. Is something wrong?" he asked, actually hoping there was so his dad wouldn't press for an answer.

"That detective fella called twice yesterday wantin' to know who else he was supposed to check out, what to do next. I had my hands full worryin' about a breech foal. Told him to talk to you, but he said he couldn't find you. Well, finally I just told him to find out about everybody and anybody connected to the murder. Just check 'em all.''

Travis had to smile. "Gonna be a helluva bill."

"Well, you was nowhere to be found, and—"

"It's okay, Dad. Sounds like a good idea, anyway. He sure hasn't turned up much so far."

"You talked to that preacher yet?"

"Priest, Dad. And no, not yet."

"Well, why the hell not? Just—"

"I'm working on it, Dad," Travis said a little too sharply.

"Sure…I know you are. It's just so damn frustrating. This all sounded so simple when we started."

"Guess what? We were wrong. Sorry if I snapped at you."

"Ah, don't pay it no never mind. Maybe Foster will come up with somethin'."

"Maybe."

"By the way, you buy a mare or not?"

"Actually, I'm thinking about buying two of them. I'm meeting with Jax Delacroix later today. I'll see if I can't tie up the sale then."

"Good. You been gone over a week. 'Bout time you hightailed it home. 'Specially since we're gettin' nowhere fast on this thing."

"If Foster hits pay dirt by tomorrow, I'll pack it in as soon as the vet gives the okay."

"Don't like it any better than you do, but we can't get to the tabloids without proof."

"Yeah, I know. See ya, Dad."

"Take care, Trav."

BEFORE LEAVING SHELBY at Riverwood shortly after sunrise, Travis had made a date with her for lunch. Now, driving back into Bayou Beltane to keep that date, he decided to swing by the park where they had first kissed, for no particular reason except that it pleased him. As he drew near the park, he glanced over at the church and saw William Delacroix tending some flower beds outside. The priest waved. Travis pulled over, parked and walked across the street.

"Hello, Travis. How are you?"

"Fine, Father, and you?"

"Thought we agreed to drop the formalities." William pulled off a gardening glove in order to shake hands.

Travis grinned. "Sorry, Father. It goes against my training. My grandmother was a no-nonsense lady when it came to manners."

"Was?"

"She died recently."

"I'm sorry to hear that. I'll say a prayer for her at mass tomorrow."

"Thanks. She raised me after my mother died and was really more of a mother than a grandmother."

"Well, looks like she did a fine job," William commented. "So, have you found the mare you were looking for?"

"Actually, I've decided to buy the first one I looked at. After Shelby and I have lunch, I've got an appointment with Jax to finalize the sale of Zaira."

William smiled. "A sweet one, our Shelby."

"About as sweet as they come," Travis agreed.

"Strong willed, too. Most of the family is. It seems every time I do research, I run across another determined ancestor."

At the mention of ancestors, an idea came to Travis—a risky idea, if William Delacroix wasn't inclined to keep confidences. But Travis's own research into his great-aunt's life and death seemed to be stymied.

"Could I ask you a question, Father?"

"Certainly."

"What folks say to you is confidential, right?"

"In the confessional, yes. As Charles mentioned at dinner the other night, I'm officially retired, so I don't hear confessions regularly, but the priesthood is not something you can really retire from. Besides, in here—" he tapped his heart "—I'm honor-bound to keep all confidences. In or out of the confessional."

Travis hesitated for several moments, then made a decision. "Then, I'd like to talk to you about something that happened in Bayou Beltane almost sixty years ago. A girl was killed—"

"Are you talking about the murder of Camille Gravier?"

Travis's heart beat faster. "Yeah. What can you tell me about it?"

"What do you want to know?"

"Anything you remember about her death, or the trial."

"Well," the priest said, taking a deep breath. "That's a tall order. I can tell you that I knew Camille Gravier. But it's not something I'm proud of."

"Excuse me?"

"I said, I'm not proud of my association with Camille Gravier. That's a time in my life that I've put behind me."

Stunned at the harshness in the priest's voice, Travis couldn't let the conversation end there. "Father, I'm not asking out of idle curiosity. This is real important to me.''

''I can see that. Do you mind if I ask why? What could possibly interest you about a crime that happened so long ago?''

''She was my great-aunt.''

Now it was William's turn to look surprised. ''Sweet heaven.''

''My grandmother was Roberta Gravier Hardin, and I came here to fulfill her dying request. Her sister was an innocent young woman—''

''Innocent? Is that what your grandmother told you?''

''Yes.''

''God bless her, she may have even believed it,'' he mumbled.

''Come again?''

''Travis, will you meet me here at the church after your lunch with Shelby?''

''Yeah, but—''

''We need more time to talk, and more privacy.''


''HEY.'' SHELBY SNAPPED her fingers.

''What?'' Travis said, his thoughts still on his conversation with William Delacroix. ''Sorry, darlin'.''

''You're a million miles away. Something wrong?''

They were headed back to her office after a return visit to Rick's Café. ''Just a problem at my ranch,'' he lied. ''Nothing serious. Just needs tending to.''

Shelby's heart almost skipped a beat. ''I...suppose that means you'll be leaving sooner than you expected?''

''No.''

She reached across the seat of the truck and touched his arm. "I know you'll leave sooner or later, but to be honest, later suits me fine."

"You don't see me in a hurry to pack my bags, do you?"

"No, thank goodness."

"And it isn't like Texas is on the other side of the world. We let foreigners come across the Louisiana border all the time."

"How gracious—oh, Travis," she suddenly said. "Do you mind stopping at the Book Nook? I have some papers in my briefcase for my client to sign. I'm not keeping you from anything, am I?"

"No." More lies. Lies upon lies. He was beginning to feel as if his life was defined by them.

He pulled over and parked in front of the bookstore, then walked around to open the door for Shelby. "I can wait in the truck—" he began.

"No. This isn't a meeting between client and attorney. I just need some signatures."

When they stepped inside the bookstore, Yvette was nowhere to be seen. A young woman, barely out of her teens, was stocking a shelf near the door with books. "Good afternoon," she said. "Can I help you find something?"

"I'm looking for the owner," Shelby told her.

"She's busy at the moment, but I'll be happy to—"

"My name is Shelby Delacroix, and I'm Ms. Avenall's attorney. It's not anything urgent, but I have some papers that require her signature."

"Oh." The young girl looked embarrassed. "I'm sorry. I thought you were a customer. Nice to meet you. My name's Liz."

Shelby smiled. "Perfectly understandable, Liz. When do you expect Yvette to return?"

"Oh, she's not gone. Some gentlemen came in a few moments ago, and she went to the back to talk to them."

Shelby was immediately alerted. "The back?"

"There's a small office back there. And the rear entrance."

Shelby turned to Travis. "My client is with some men who may be...difficult. If I need your help—"

"You won't even have to turn around, darlin'. I'm right with you."

When they stepped into the office, which was scarcely more than a closet, they found it empty and the door leading to the alley wide open. Shelby didn't pause but walked straight through.

"Yvette?"

Yvette's head snapped around. "Sh-Shelby? I—I didn't know you were here."

Two men—one tall, bald and built like a wrestler, the other wearing mirrored sunglasses—had Shelby's friend backed up against the outside wall of the bookstore. She was visibly trembling.

"Am I interrupting?" Shelby asked, approaching the three.

"I, uh—"

"We were just talking to Ms. Avenall here," the bald man said.

"Indeed. Are these men friends of yours, Yvette?"

"No."

"Are you process servers?" Shelby asked.

Travis, right behind her, heard the edge in her voice. He didn't know what was going on, but he sure as hell didn't like it. Or the look of the two men.

Expensive suits or not, he recognized muscle when he saw it. He moved closer to Shelby. This was her client and her play, as long as the dressed-up muscle didn't get pushy.

"Who's asking?" the man with the mirrored sunglasses added.

"I am."

"And who are you?"

"Ms. Avenall's attorney. And unless you're interested in buying a book, I suggest you find somewhere else to loiter."

Baldy cut his partner a pointed look. "We were just leaving, anyway."

They moved away from Yvette in the direction of the alley that led to the street, but Shelby was quicker and had planted herself squarely in their path. Suddenly, Travis realized she intended to confront these men.

"Gentlemen," she said before he had a chance to stop her. "I have one other suggestion. And you may want to pass this on to whomever signs your paychecks. Don't bother Ms. Avenall again."

When Baldy looked Shelby up and down, Travis moved closer still. He was at her back and ready to move her, bodily if need be, out of harm's way. The tension in the alley was thick as a Panhandle dust storm.

"We weren't bothering anybody, were we?" Sunglasses said.

"No," Baldy told her. "We were just trying to make Ms. Avenall aware of all her...options." He moved toward Shelby, but Travis was faster.

"You want to talk options? Talk to me."

Baldly looked at Shelby. "This your guard dog?"

"Count on it," Travis replied.

For several seconds, Baldy studied Travis, then with a nod to Sunglasses they walked out of the alley.

Travis heard Shelby's sigh of relief as he grabbed her by the shoulders and spun her around to face him. "What the hell do you think you're doing?"

"My job."

"You're a lawyer, not a member of a SWAT team."

"I'm an officer of the court. And what about you—"

At that moment Yvette came rushing over to them. "Shelby, I was so scared. I can't believe you stood up to them the way you did."

Travis scowled at Shelby. "Neither can I."

"Bullies," she told them. "Get rid of the expensive suits and sunglasses and that's all you've got. Overgrown bullies."

"Did it ever occur to you that those overgrown bullies might be carrying guns?" Travis demanded.

"Guns?" the women said in unison.

"Oh, Shelby," Yvette cried. "I'd never forgive myself if anything happened to you on my account."

"And I'd never forgive myself if I didn't protect you to the best of my ability."

"Without body armor?" Travis growled.

Shelby glared at him. "Travis…"

"I mean it, Shelby. That was a damned fool thing to do."

"I beg your pardon…" She took a deep breath. "Why are we standing in an alley arguing about this?"

"Because you're fearless and don't know when to back off?"

She was trying not to lose her temper, but he was making it hard. "Let's go inside." She gestured for Yvette to go ahead of her. "We'll talk about this later," she said over her shoulder.

"Damn straight," Travis replied.

They walked back into the bookstore, and he made sure the rear entrance was locked securely.

"Could I use your phone?" Shelby asked once they were again in the front of the store.

"Sure," Yvette replied.

Shelby walked to the counter, flipped open her briefcase, then her address book. She found the telephone number she was looking for, closed the briefcase and dialed.

"Walter Trowbridge, please. Tell him Shelby Delacroix is calling. I see," she said. "Well then, give him a message, please, for his client. Call off the goons. He'll know what I mean."

She hung up and immediately dialed her own office, asking for her secretary.

"She's amazing," Yvette said.

"Amazing." Travis wrestled with the chauvinistic urge to grab Shelby and whisk her off to someplace safe. But as he listened to her giving instructions to her office, watched her calmly go about the business of providing her client with the best legal representation she could, he realized she *was* amazing. Shelby didn't think of herself as extraordinary, but she was. She was also the best thing that had ever happened to him, and he couldn't imagine what his life would be like without her.

Yvette looked up at Travis. "She's lucky to have you."

Still watching Shelby, he shoved his hands into the

pockets of his jeans. "Believe me. The luck is all mine." But for how long? he wondered. How long?

"Well," Shelby said, hanging up the phone, "I'm sorry for the delay. Yvette, I brought some papers for you to sign. There's no rush. You can drop them by the office later this afternoon, or even tomorrow."

"I'll sign them now."

"Not until you've read them. Never sign anything until you've read it," she cautioned, smiling. "Not even from your attorney."

"If you say so."

"I do." She gave her friend a reassuring pat on the shoulder. "Call me if you have any questions." Then she turned to Travis. "Ready to go?" He nodded and they left the store.

He didn't say another word until he pulled up in front of her office. After killing the engine, he turned to her and just stared.

"Travis? What's the matter?"

"Nothing."

"You look so…serious," she told him.

"Serious about…" No, he wasn't going to profess his love sitting in a truck in front of her office in the middle of the day. She deserved better. "About taking you out on the town tonight."

"Nope. Too public."

"But—"

"You don't get it, do you, cowboy." She kissed him lightly on the mouth. "I don't want to share you with cocktail waitresses and maître d's. I want you all to myself. Seven o'clock. Your motel. I'll bring the pizza." She grabbed a handful of his shirt and pulled him to her for a quick, hard kiss. "Be there."

TRAVIS WAS SO RATTLED by the realization that he loved Shelby that he completely forgot about meeting Father William. In fact, he almost forgot about his appointment with Jax, as well. He managed to keep the appointment to finalize the sale of the mare and make arrangements for transportation, but for the life of him he couldn't remember a single detail afterward.

What did horses and ancient history matter when he was in love with Shelby Delacroix?

He could already see the look on his father's face when he brought Shelby home to meet him. *Dad, this is the woman I love, Shelby Delacroix. You remember the name Delacroix, don't you? Those people involved in murdering Gran's sister?*

The fact that Travis was even thinking in terms of introducing Shelby to his father was proof positive of how far the situation had deteriorated. What hope was there for any kind of relationship once Shelby learned the truth? She would hate him.

The thought sent cold chills down his spine. He had just realized he loved her, and now he would have to get used to the idea of her hating him. Fate was cruel.

And she was coming to him tonight, expecting to share herself the way she had practically from the moment they'd met. Expecting to share her heart. Expecting him to accept her gift of love.

Maybe he could derail her somehow, he thought. Insist they go out for dinner. Wine and dine her... Who was he kidding? Derail Shelby? Not when she only knew one direction—straight ahead; one speed, flat out.

Who *was* he kidding? Telling himself he couldn't

derail Shelby sounded like an excellent excuse to do what he wanted to do. Be with her. Love her. If only for one last time.

There was a knock on the door, and when he opened it, there stood Shelby, wearing jeans and that outrageously sexy little peek-a-boo sweater, holding a pizza box in one hand, a six-pack of long necks in the other. How was he supposed to resist all that sass, sex and love wrapped up in one beautiful package? It simply wasn't possible.

"You look like a purist to me. Pepperoni, extra cheese." She eyed him over the box. "No anchovies. No onions."

"Do I have to tip you?"

Moving faster than he expected, she stepped inside, set the pizza and beer on a nearby table and threw herself into his arms so hard he almost lost his balance. "Oh, brother, do you ever," she said as she kissed him.

"How do you feel about cold pizza?"

"If we hurry, it'll still be warm."

"Oh, no. Not this time," he said, running his hands up and down the sides of her body. "My style, remember?"

"Something about slow and easy."

"Yeah." He traced her bottom lip with his tongue and smiled when she slipped her hand down to his hip, urging him closer. "I seem to recall you said, 'next time.'"

"Did I?"

"Guess what?"

"Hmm?"

"It's this time."

"If you insist, but—"

"I'll do more than insist. I'll coax, persuade, then I'll show you just how slow, just how easy making love should be. There won't be anything else but me touching you, kissing you, wanting you. And you wanting me. But the wanting will be sweet and hot."

"Travis," she whispered as his tongue danced up her throat. Her body was already trembling with need.

"I'm glad you wore this sweater," he said.

"Why?"

"Because when you had it on the other night—" he unbuttoned the first two buttons "—I almost went crazy every time I caught a glimpse of bare skin." The last of the buttons gave way, and he pushed the sweater over her shoulders and down her arms. He flung it into a chair.

Struggling against the urge to rush, he cupped her breasts in his hands. She sighed.

"See? Slow and sweet." While he unhooked her lace bra from the back, he kissed the swell of her breasts. The bra went the way of the sweater. "So sweet." He savored her soft flesh, his tongue flicking across her nipple until it was hard.

"H-how…" She squirmed, barely able to breathe. "How slow does it have to be?"

"Very."

She clutched at his shirt. "Travis, I need…"

"I know, and you'll have it." He carried her to the bed. "Eventually."

And he was as good as his word. He drove her slowly to the edge of madness while exploring every delicious inch of her body. He easily made her wild with need. And when she begged for him to end her torment, he refused. Until finally he drove himself mad, too. Until finally slow and easy had no choice but to be fast and hard. But even then he made her soar, made her feel treasured beyond measure. Loved beyond dreams.

# CHAPTER TWELVE

HE'D THOUGHT ABOUT it most of the night—at least what was left of it after Shelby went home. He had rehearsed what he was going to say, and imagined a hundred ways she might respond. Now, leaving the Slidell city limits behind on his way to meet Shelby for breakfast, he was ready to call off his plan.

*Plan.*

The word implied he knew what he was doing, what he hoped to accomplish. Yeah, right. A plan was what had got him into trouble in the first place. This idea of his to present Shelby with a hypothetical situation in order to see how she would respond had sounded fine when he first conceived it. But the more he thought about it, the less sure he was of success. He couldn't seem to come up with anything else that might give Shelby an opportunity to assess his predicament, however. Hypothetically, of course.

Travis parked outside the café, then went inside to wait for her. "Hey there, darlin'," he said when she approached the table ten minutes later.

"Hey there, yourself."

"I ordered you some coffee." He picked up a small bowl containing individual servings of cream and set it in front of her. He did the same with the sugar container. "One spoonful of sugar, lots of cream."

Smiling, Shelby added two creams and reached for

the sugar. "You're a jewel. I still say the women in Texas need to have their heads examined for letting you run around loose all these years." She took a drink of the coffee and sighed. "Boy, did I need this."

"Restless night?" he teased.

She gazed at him over the rim of her cup. "I'm not complaining."

"Yeah, all that legal maneuvering must be hard work. Late-night negotiations and everything."

"Depends on the maneuvers." Discreetly, so that none of the other patrons in the café could see, she crossed her legs and stroked his calf with the side of her foot.

"I trust everything worked out in your favor."

"Oh, yes. I was very satisfied with the outcome. In fact—" she leaned forward, lowering her voice "—it was absolutely the most satisfying night of…"

Travis cleared his throat and picked up his menu as the waitress approached. After she had taken their order and left, Shelby whispered, "Behave yourself."

"Me? I wasn't the one playing footsie under the table."

"But it's your fault."

"And just how do you figure that?"

"Because you're so darned sexy."

"Oh, well." He grinned. "Then, you're right, it was my fault."

This time she rapped his leg with her foot. "Hey." He rubbed his shin. "Why don't we talk about something less—"

"Physical?"

Travis grinned. "So, what's cookin' for you today?"

"Researching a case for my cousin Joanna."

"Something interesting, or can you even talk about it?"

"Yes. And no, of course I can't talk about it."

Toying with his coffee cup, Travis decided if he was going to put his plan into action, it was now or never. "Have you ever defended someone accused of murder?"

"Lord, no."

"Why do you say it like that?"

"Because I don't have enough experience to try a murder case."

"Aw, c'mon, darlin', with your brains and good looks you'd make one helluva Perry Mason."

"Only in fiction."

"Seriously," he said. "Until I ran into you I didn't have much use for lawyers."

"Because?"

The phrase *Oh, what a tangled web we weave* skittered through his mind, but he shoved it aside, took a deep breath and started his make-believe tale. "A friend's whole life was messed up because of a lawyer."

"What happened?"

"Hank—that's my friend's name—his father was accused of murdering his first wife thirty years after the fact."

"Thirty years?"

Travis nodded. "She was strangled to death, and her then lover was tried, convicted and sentenced to hang. The lover claimed to be innocent from the beginning, and he finally got so depressed he committed suicide in his cell. Thirty years later, the man's daughter decided Hank's dad was the real killer. She was out for revenge and didn't care who got hurt along the way.''

"Was…was she right?''

Travis wondered if Shelby was asking as the tenderhearted woman he'd made love to last night or as a lawyer. "No one knows.''

"Why not?''

"The police questioned Hank's dad, then released him due to lack of evidence. But the girl later turned up some facts that hadn't been brought out at the trial. For one thing, the dead woman had been stealing from Hank's dad, and he found out the day she died. He was mad as hell. For another, it looked like the judge had been bribed. In the end, they couldn't prove Hank's dad killed her any more than they could prove the other guy hadn't. Hank's mom was blindly loyal to his dad, but Hank wasn't so sure. He ended up hating the guy's daughter for stirring it all up, and hating his father for keeping his past a secret. It tore their family up.''

"Oh, Travis. I'm so sorry for your friend. That's tragic. Unfortunately, the system isn't perfect, and occasionally it fails.''

"Yeah? How would you feel in Hank's shoes?''

She cocked her head to one side and thought for a moment. "Truthfully? I don't know.'' She shrugged. "Who's to say that Hank's father wasn't violent and aggressive as a young man? Hank might not have seen it, but then, people have a tendency to mellow as they get older. On the other hand, I'm not sure I could continue a relationship with someone I thought was capable of killing *and* had allowed another man to die for a crime he'd committed. As for the hatred…the daughter was justified, if she thought an injustice had been done. Unfortunately, Hank and his family suffered in the process. It sounds like everybody lost in this situation.''

Travis stared at her, awed again by her integrity and powerful sense of fairness. ''Yeah,'' he said, raising his cup of coffee for a drink. ''That's for damn sure.''

But her words gave him hope. ''Too bad all lawyers aren't like you, darlin'.''

''Hmm. Even lawyers love flattery.''

''So sue me. I think you're terrific.''

''I think you're terrific right back.''

He set his cup down and looked into her eyes. ''I'd just about given up on ever finding a woman like you.''

''Well, I'm sure glad you didn't stop looking.''

''Yeah. Me, too.'' He reached across the table and linked his hand with hers. ''Me, too.''

TRAVIS PULLED UP IN FRONT of the church and parked, but he didn't get out. William Delacroix was waiting for him inside, waiting to talk to him about the past. Travis glanced down. Beside him on the seat was a manila envelope containing copies of the letters written by Camille to Gran.

Travis should be pleased, even excited that he was finally about to get some answers to the many questions concerning Camille's death. This was the reason he'd come to Bayou Beltane in the first place. This was what he had promised Gran. And after his conversation with Shelby over breakfast, he had even more reason to think that eventually they could be together without the shadow of the past hanging over them. Yeah. He should be pleased.

Then, why did he feel like a traitor?

Because he didn't want to hurt her. He didn't want to ever be responsible for causing her one moment's pain.

Last night he had held Shelby in his arms, understanding for the first time how much he loved her, needed her. And how loving and needing would change his life. Had already changed his life.

He glanced over at the entrance to the church and for a second, maybe two, considered not going in. Not talking to Father William. In the end, Travis knew he had to do it. But he also knew the sting of revenge was gone from his heart, no matter what the retired priest told him. Loving Shelby had taken it away. He got out of his car and went inside, but his quest was no longer a matter of reclaiming family honor.

It was a matter of setting the record straight so that he could face the woman he loved with honesty.

"Hello," Father William said when Travis stepped inside the sanctuary.

"I appreciate you seeing me, especially since I missed our appointment yesterday."

"Come with me," the priest requested, and headed out of the chapel to a small courtyard. "Please…" He motioned for Travis to have a seat on the cast-stone bench beneath a tree dripping with Spanish moss.

"It's mighty nice of you to—"

"Let's get something clear right now. I don't like having to relive a part of my past that I would rather forget. But I feel the truth is important. You do want the truth, don't you, Travis?"

"That's why I came to Bayou Beltane."

"I take it Shelby doesn't know about any of this, or who you are."

Travis cleared his throat. "You're right."

"I thought so. She's not going to be happy when she learns you've lied to her."

"I haven't exactly—"

"Young man," William said sternly. "If we're here to deal with the truth, then don't start with self-justification."

Travis had the good grace to be ashamed. "You…you said you knew my great-aunt."

William took a deep breath. "I did, indeed."

"Did you know her well?"

"Too well. I rue the day I ever met her."

"Why?"

William looked down at his hands folded in his lap. "Travis, you won't like what I've got to say. I don't mean to hurt you with the things I'm about to tell you, but often the truth is painful."

Somewhere in the back of his mind, Travis remembered almost the exact same words coming from his grandmother, but they had been intended as an admonition. Somehow he didn't think that's what Father William had in mind. "Whatever the truth is, I want to hear it."

"All right. Camille Gravier was no good. She was vain, selfish and self-centered. Looking back, I've wondered if her soul wasn't already lost to Satan before I ever met her." At the hard look in Travis's eyes, he said, "I told you that you wouldn't like what I had to say.

"She collected men the way some girls collect dolls. They were a means to an end for her. Money, position, whatever she wanted she got by using a man. She preferred rich men, but even poor Rafe Perdido didn't escape her devastating charms. I use the word *devastating* because any man who was stupid enough, or lovesick enough, to think she cared for him was sadly mistaken.''

Travis shot up from the bench. ''I've heard enough! Your whole family was involved in her murder right up to your eyebrows. You've got a helluva lot of nerve trashing my great-aunt when she can't defend herself. Why, you sanctimonious old…'' He forced himself to breathe deeply, forced himself to get control of his temper.

''Look,'' Travis continued when he was calmer. ''I figure the way you see the thing is bound to be colored by your calling. Moral judgments are your business. But where do you get off passing on gossip as first-hand information?''

''What makes you think it's gossip?''

''It's not like you ever had anything to do with Camille.''

''You think I was born a priest?'' William shook his head. ''Camille was my test of faith.'' He closed his eyes, then opened them and looked directly at Travis. ''And I failed.''

''I—I…'' Stunned, Travis didn't know quite how to respond. ''I find this hard to believe.''

''Understandable. But I can give you the names of at least five other people who would probably tell you very similar stories about Camille. Why would I lie?''

''To protect your brother.''

''Brother? Don't you mean brothers? She slept with both Charles and Philip. I'm not certain, but I feel sure she slept with Rafe Perdido, as well.''

Travis shook his head. This was too much. The priest couldn't be telling the truth.

"Please…" William again indicated the bench. "You'll take all of this better sitting down." Numbly Travis did as he suggested.

"I was seventeen and on my second visit home from the seminary when I met Camille and fell hopelessly in love with her. She was beautiful, charming, graceful.… I never expected to respond to a woman so forcefully, so passionately. Determined to stay on guard against temptation, I tried to keep away from her. But it was no use. I was drawn to her like the proverbial moth to a flame. She was so vibrant, so compelling, I—I just couldn't resist her. It made no difference when I was warned she only wanted a piece of the Delacroix fortune." William rubbed the bridge of his nose with his thumb and finger. "Eventually, I questioned my dedication to the church. To everything but her. Then I found out she had been sleeping with not only Charles, but Philip, as well. I was devastated." He looked at Travis. "And yes, angry. I hated her. But I didn't kill her. Rafe Perdido did."

"I…it's—"

"Unbelievable?"

"Yes."

"I've just confessed something to you that has been a black spot on my soul for almost sixty years. Ask yourself why I would save my family's name rather than my immortal soul."

"My grandmother always told me how sweet, how innocent her sister was."

"Roberta, wasn't it? She was in the same class as

Charles and Philip. I remember her as a very serious girl. Responsible.''

"But she must have suspected the Delacroix were responsible for the ruin of our family. That's obvious from Camille's letters.''

"Well, I'm ashamed to say that's partly true. My father, Hamilton, fired your great-grandfather from the timber mill. Word got out, and Gravier couldn't get a job. He finally left the state.''

"The family moved to Texas," Travis said, still trying to absorb all William had told him.

"You know, in defense of Roberta, I think she saw Camille as much more than she was. Forgive me, but your grandmother was a plain woman, where as Camille was almost breathtakingly beautiful. Maybe, over the years, Roberta needed to remember her sister as innocent and gullible in order to deal with the loss.''

How ironic, Travis thought. His dad had said almost the same thing.

"You came to Bayou Beltane looking for revenge, didn't you?''

"Yeah.''

"And what were you planning to do with your so-called truth? Hand it over to the district attorney so he could reopen an ancient murder case?''

"No. I figured the Delacroix might buy him off.''

"Then, how did you—''

"I was going to hand over the information to a newspaper.''

"A tabloid?''

When Travis didn't answer, William nodded. "I assume you've dug through the old newspaper files.'' Travis nodded. "Talked to people?''

"Not many."

"And have you found any new evidence?"

Travis thought about the letters and the baby. But was the baby Charles's, or could it have been Philip's or Rafe's?

Travis considered telling the priest, then changed his mind. What good would it serve now? If what William said was true, there was no way to prove who the baby's father was, any more than there was a way to prove who had murdered Camille. If William was lying...

But why would he lie?

In the last few minutes something Travis had thought was the truth had been shot full of holes. But he couldn't just dismiss everything Gran had told him. William's tale sounded like the truth, but Travis couldn't just accept it and turn his back on his promise. Neither could he add to William's obvious burden of a long-ago sin.

"No," he finally told William. "I didn't find any new evidence."

"You don't think very highly of us, do you. With the exception of Shelby, of course."

"Shelby," Travis whispered.

"Yes. Sweet, trusting Shelby. She'll have to learn who you are."

"Got no right to ask this, considering what I've just told you, but I'd appreciate it if you didn't say anything to her."

"Only if you tell her yourself."

"I'm not sure about anything except..." Travis turned pleading eyes to the priest. "Except that I love her."

"Well," William said, "that's a good place to start."

All that mattered was his love for Shelby. Travis kept telling himself that as he shook William Delacroix's hand and left the church. He would find a way to tell her, and pray that she was forgiving. But first he wanted to clear away the past completely. That meant going back to Texas and explaining everything to his father.

Driving to Shelby's office, Travis realized he needed to talk to his dad, but that this was not the kind of news to be delivered over the phone. Neither was the news that he was in love with Shelby and intended to marry her if she would have him. T. C. Hardin was a fair man, but this was a lot to ask. Travis was having enough trouble weeding through everything himself; he dreaded to think how his dad would react. But, like facing Shelby with the truth, Travis had to confront him.

The future was uppermost in his mind as Travis walked into the law offices of Delacroix and Associates and asked for Shelby. A few seconds later she came down the hall.

She smiled the instant she saw him. "Hi. I didn't expect to see you until tonight."

"New plans, darlin'. Gotta head home."

Her smiled faded. "Oh."

"You're way off, counselor." He glanced around and noticed that a couple of secretaries could easily overhear what he had to say. "C'mon. I need to talk to you in private."

"Sure," Shelby said, her heart aching as she followed him outside.

Once on the sidewalk, he reached into his pocket

and withdrew a key chain holding two keys. He took one off and gave it to Shelby.

"What's this?"

"Would you believe it's the key to my heart?"

Her gaze flew to his. "What?"

"Actually, it's the other key to my motel room in Slidell. I want to you keep it."

"I don't understand—"

"No time to explain everything, darlin'. The most important thing is that I'm coming back, Shelby. Just as soon as I trailer the mares to Comfort and…well, take care of some business. But I will be back, and when I do, I gotta talk to you, Shelby."

"About what?"

"Things" was all he said. "Important things." He closed her fingers over the key. "Will you wait for me?"

As if she hadn't been waiting for this man all her life. She smiled and threw her arms around his neck, not caring who saw or who gossiped. "I'll be right here, cowboy," she told him as she pulled his head down for a passionate kiss.

"I'll hurry."

# CHAPTER THIRTEEN

IT WAS WELL AFTER DARK when Shelby arrived home. She had worked a long day, more to keep herself from missing Travis than attempting to catch up on her workload. She was tired and hungry, having skipped dinner. And lonely. Glancing at her watch as she got out of the car, she realized that Travis would be home by now. He had been gone less than twelve hours, and she missed him desperately. *Please let him call,* she prayed. Even long distance, the sound of his voice would be sweet music, she thought as her foot touched the first step leading to the front porch.

"Well, there you are. I was beginning to think you weren't ever coming home."

"Dad," Shelby exclaimed, thrilled to see her father. He and Jax were sitting on a wrought-iron bench at one end of the veranda.

"Hi, sweetheart." Justin Delacroix rose and greeted his second youngest daughter with a warm embrace.

"When did you get home?" she asked, hugging him back.

"About an hour ago. Jax was just telling me two mares were sold in the last few days. Your brother will be ecstatic."

"I sometimes think the bottom line is the only

thing that makes Beau's heart beat faster. He needs a good woman.''

"Well, this doesn't hurt the bottom line." Jax held up the two bills of sale.

"His name is Travis Hardin," Shelby told her father.

"Who?"

"The man who bought the mares."

"Travis Gravier Hardin, to be precise," Jax said.

"How did you know his middle name?" Shelby asked.

"From his credit report. Nowadays they give us everything but shoe size. It's standard procedure for buyers. After all, we're talking healthy sums for Delacroix Thoroughbreds.''

"Gravier?" Justin frowned. "That name sounds familiar. Do they live in the parish?"

"Texas," Shelby said, grinning. "He has a profitable quarter-horse ranch in the Hill Country, and he wanted the mares to start a line of polo ponies.''

"You seem to know a lot about him."

"Not enough." Shelby kissed her father on the cheek. "Not nearly enough, but I'm working on it.''

After Shelby breezed into the house, Justin looked at Jax. "Is there something I need to know?"

"To be perfectly honest, Dad, I haven't the vaguest idea," she said. Then she, too, kissed him on the cheek. "Good to have you home. I'll say goodnight.''

"Good night, dear," he said, and went inside.

Shelby was in the kitchen when Justin caught up with her, and she was humming. "And just when will I have the pleasure of meeting this Texan?"

"In a couple of days," she said, pouring herself a

glass of wine. She held up the bottle. "Care to join me?"

"Please."

She filled another glass and handed it to him, then went to make herself a sandwich. "He had to transport the mares, but he'll be back."

"Can I assume from the rosy glow in your cheeks that this Travis Hardin is not merely a casual acquaintance?"

"He most certainly isn't casual."

"Did you say he's planning on buying another mare?"

In the process of slathering mayonnaise on bread for a ham sandwich, Shelby glanced at her father. "He isn't coming back for more horses, Dad. He's coming back for me. At least, I think so."

"To declare his intentions and court you properly, I hope."

"Oh, Dad!" Shelby laughed. "One of the things I love most about you is that you are hopelessly old-fashioned. And to answer your question...I sure hope so."

"I see," Justin replied in the age-old parental tone of voice that implied reservation, possibly even disapproval.

Shelby was prepared for it. "I doubt it, but that's okay. Travis may not always know which fork to use, but he's got the essentials down pat."

"And those would be?"

"For one, he doesn't care what my last name is. In fact, we kissed before he ever knew I was a Delacroix. That may not sound like an essential to you, but it is to me."

"I don't know if I'm comfortable hearing my daughter talk about kissing a man."

Shelby leaned against the kitchen counter and looked her father in the eyes. "Better get used to it, because I love him."

"And how does Mr. Hardin feel about you?"

"The same, I think."

"Are you aware that's the second time you've used 'I think'? Obviously you're uncertain of your feelings. Or his. And if you're not sure of—"

"Objection, Your Honor. The prosecution is deliberately badgering the witness."

Justin took a deep breath, releasing it slowly. "Forgive me. My protective-father mode went into overdrive."

Shelby smiled. "I like your protective-father mode, but in this case, it's not warranted."

"I wouldn't like to see you get hurt."

"Neither would I, but you know what? If that happens, and I'm not saying it will," she quickly added, "it's still better than having a life without the joy of loving."

"Well, it may not be conventional, or socially well-timed, but I've always admired your drive." He clinked his glass against hers. "Here's to you, sweetheart."

"Thanks, Dad. I know you may have some reservations, but once you meet Travis, they'll vanish like they never existed. I think you two will get along famously." She picked up her sandwich and took a small bite.

"Dare I ask what your grandfather thinks of your beau?"

"It's hard to tell with Granddad. But Uncle William seems to like Travis a lot. As a matter of fact, while Travis was roaming around the parish looking at prospective mares, he did some research on a branch of his family that used to live here.''

"Is that so? What's the last name?''

"Schmidt. He didn't find anything, though.''

Justin thought for a moment. "I believe there used to be several families by that name living near Slidell, but that was years ago.''

"I'll mention it to Travis. Better yet, you can tell him yourself. I hope you'll be able to join us for dinner when Travis returns.''

"I'd love to.''

"That way you can size him up for yourself,'' she teased, knowing full well that was exactly what was going through his head.

"Scamp. Pour me a little more wine and tell me what else has been going on while I was in Baton Rouge.''

"Not much. Oh, Yvette Avenall is back in town. You remember her from when we were in high school?''

"Vaguely.''

"Well, she has a little boy now, and she's opened a bookstore down by the old depot.''

"I hope it's successful.''

"Me, too. She's really working—''

The ringing of the phone interrupted her, and Shelby all but leaped to answer it. "Hello.''

Justin didn't need to ask who was on the other end of the line. His daughter's smile was answer enough.

"Dad, would you hang up the phone when I go upstairs?''

"Certainly.''

She handed him the receiver and dashed off. He held it just close enough to his ear to be able to hear her voice when she picked up the extension. ''Thanks, Dad,'' she finally said. It took most of Justin's considerable willpower not to eavesdrop.

''Hey, darlin','' Travis said as soon as he heard the disconnecting click of the other phone.

''I was hoping you would call.'' She lay back on the bed.

''Would have called sooner, but it took some work to get those mares settled in. Did I hear you speak to your dad?''

''Yes. He came home today.''

''Guess you were glad to see him, huh?''

''Yes. But not nearly as glad as I am to hear your voice.''

There was a pause, then she heard him sigh. ''Aw, Shelby, I miss you.''

''Me too, you. I walked around in a kind of fog all day missing you.''

''Be careful, darlin'. I want you in one piece when I get back.''

''I like that.''

''What?''

''The way you said 'be careful.' ''

''Yeah? One hair-raising near miss was enough. And no more rumbles in alleys until I'm there for backup.''

''When will that be?''

''Tomorrow.''

Now it was Shelby's turn to sigh. ''Thank goodness. What time?''

''Around six-thirty.''

Shelby sat straight up on the bed. "In the morning?" she asked hopefully.

"Sorry, darlin'. That's p.m., not a.m. I've got to tie up some loose ends here before I can leave."

She moaned. "I don't like it, but I guess I'll live."

"I'll head straight for Riverwood."

Shelby reached into the pocket of her skirt, her fingers brushing the key to his motel room in Slidell. She smiled. "I've got a better idea."

"Darlin', there isn't a better idea than you and me gettin' together as soon as possible."

"But not at Riverwood. I'll meet you at your motel. In fact, I'll be waiting for you in the room."

"Like I said the first time we met, I do love a lady who knows her own mind."

They talked for almost an hour, about her day, his trip. About the weather in Texas. Neither seemed to care how inconsequential the topic so long as they could hear each other's voice. Finally, Travis could tell that Shelby was fading.

"Darlin', you need some shut-eye," he told her.

"I'd rest a lot better if you were beside me."

"If I were beside you, neither of us would be getting any sleep, and you know it."

"You're right," she said with a yawn.

"Good night, darlin'. Sweet dreams."

"Good night. I love you," she said as she hung up the receiver.

"Shelby, I—" the connection was broken "—love you."

She hadn't heard him, but that was all right. The next time he talked to her she would hear the words. He would tell her how much he loved her. He only prayed her love for him was strong enough to survive finding out who he was.

THE NEXT MORNING Justin was finishing breakfast when Shelby came downstairs.

"Good morning," he said warmly.

Shelby stretched and yawned. "Morning. You playing golf today?" she asked, noticing he was dressed casually.

"Yes. Why don't you meet me for lunch at the club?"

"Can't. Alan Renquist and I are having a working lunch."

Justin's mention of the country club reminded Shelby of something Yvette had told her regarding Lyle Masson and his cronies. "Hey, Dad. Do you know Lyle Masson?"

"Not well. And I prefer it that way."

"He's got a questionable reputation?"

"Questionable enough to make me want to keep my distance."

"What have you heard?"

Justin looked at his daughter. "This sudden interest in Masson wouldn't be professional, by any chance?"

"Have you ever heard of anything called the Men's Club?"

"Why do you ask? And you didn't answer my question, Shelby. Please tell me you haven't taken Lyle Masson on as a client."

"Lord, no. Just the opposite. You sure the Men's Club doesn't ring any bells?"

"There are a lot of men's clubs—"

"No. The Men's Club. Probably Lyle and four or five power types, including Uncle Philip?"

"Philip?"

"Yep. And I have a hunch these guys don't meet for coffee and beignets."

"Where did you get this information?" At her arched eyebrow, he nodded. "I see. Privileged."

"If you hear anything about this obscure little group, will you let me know?"

"Of course, but as a federal judge, you know I can't afford to get too nosy. Besides, if Philip is involved, you can rest assured not everything is as it appears. Have you asked your grandfather about this club?"

"No. Actually, I just remembered it a moment ago. But that's a good idea."

"Just because Dad and Uncle Philip don't speak unless it's at Aunt Mary's house of an absolute necessity, that doesn't mean Dad doesn't keep tabs on his brother. He will be more help than I was."

"Thanks."

"I don't suppose you'll be home for dinner tonight?" Justin asked.

"No, I won't. Or breakfast, either."

"Thank you, but that was more information than I needed to know."

Shelby opened a drawer and retrieved a plastic bag, then took a bagel from a platter on the table. "Just letting you know so you won't worry. I'm being a responsible adult."

He cleared his throat. "Speaking of being responsible…"

"Don't worry, Daddy. I got all the birds-and-bees information back in seventh-grade health class. And I'm taking care of myself."

"Well…good." Justin shifted his weight from one foot to the other.

Shelby zipped the bag closed. "Got to run. See you later." And she dashed off.

"HEY, TRAV." T.C. NUDGED his sleeping son. "You drove most of the night, and you've damn near slept the mornin' away. You got a call."

Travis rolled over and yawned. "What?"

"Foster's on the line," T.C. announced, and handed him the extension phone.

Sleepy eyed, Travis grappled with the receiver as T.C. left the room. "Foster?"

"Mr. Hardin. I received the directive from your father, and I'm sorry I've been a few days getting back to you, but gathering dossiers on three additional subjects takes a little time. Particularly since it required going so far back."

"Which three?"

"Judge Neville Alvarez, Rafael Perdido and, uh—" Foster cleared his throat "—Camille Gravier."

"You checked up on my great-aunt? What the hell—"

"Your father instructed me to do 'everybody.' From the day you hired me, I've been in contact with you *and* your father on all information. And since, technically, I was hired by both of you—"

"Yeah, yeah. I got it, Foster. Your butt's covered."

"Thank you. I've faxed—"

"What's the story on Alvarez?"

"These are just highlights, understand. Nothing much on the judge except that he seemed to have an eye for the ladies and spent a lot of money on them.

Had several mistresses over the years, one a long-term affair. Got a substantial amount of his income from 'campaign supporters' such as some of the oil companies, and from friends in state politics. A few bribes, but they wouldn't even raise an eyebrow in today's political climate. Oh, and he was a personal friend of Hamilton Delacroix.''

"And Perdido?''

"Skimpy. Had some family in Maryland, but they all scattered after World War I. Pretty much the man the newspapers painted him to be. A quick-tempered drifter but real hot with the babes.''

There was a long silence while Travis tried to decide if he wanted to hear intimate details of his great-aunt's life. He kept remembering Gran telling him stories about her.

Then he remembered Father William using words like *vain, selfish* and *self-centered* to describe her. And the look on his face when he'd said, *Camille was my test of faith. And I failed.*

"What about my great-aunt?''

"Mr. Hardin, I'd rather you read the report—''

"Go ahead, Foster.''

The detective cleared his throat again. "From all accounts she was beautiful. Finished high school, but barely. Worked at the Delacroix timber mill office for a while—''

"Think that's where she met Charles?''

"Actually, she already knew him through his sister, Mary. Uh, Charles got her the job. She didn't stay long, moved on to the five-and-dime in downtown Bayou Beltane. Dated local young men, but only ones with money or position, or both. She spent a fair amount of time at a blues joint just outside of town.

Kinda seedy, a leftover speakeasy from Prohibition. That's where she met Perdido.''

''Define 'dated.' ''

''Pardon?''

''She 'dated local young men'... What does that mean?''

Foster hesitated for a second, then said, ''She had a reputation for being what was referred to in those days as loose.''

Travis held on to a frail hope. ''Could have been gossip.''

''You'll have to judge for yourself, Mr. Hardin. The documentation is extensive.''

There was another long silence. ''Send everything you've collected to me, along with your bill. Fax me the last three reports.''

''Of course. Now, I called your motel in Slidell this morning, and they informed me you were still registered there.''

''I'm going back today.''

''Then, there's no problem. I appreciate your business, Mr. Hardin.''

Travis hung up the receiver and ran a hand over his stubbled cheek. He'd had a helluva trip home last night accompanied by a line of thunderstorms. It had taken three hours longer than he'd expected, and he was beat. Now he had to pull himself together and explain everything that had happened to his dad. Including Shelby.

DURING THE DAY, Shelby tried several times to reach Yvette at the bookstore, but Liz answered each time, saying her boss was running an errand or had gone to pick up Dante. Masson's attorney had called

Shelby with a new settlement offer, and she wanted to discuss it with Yvette. Shelby's instincts told her something wasn't quite right, but she couldn't identify the cause of her concern.

One thing was for certain—waiting for Travis was going to make it a long day.

As it turned out, the time went much faster than she expected. Her luncheon meeting with Alan was wonderfully productive, and afterward she finally came to the decision to concentrate her practice on family law. She couldn't wait to tell Travis about her decision. After tonight, she hoped to share everything about her life, her career, with him.

*Travis. Travis. Travis.*

How could she be so lucky to have found a man like him? she wondered as she pulled into the parking lot of his motel. He was everything she wanted in a man—honest, ambitious and sexy beyond belief. He was smart and funny. And she loved him totally, completely, with all her heart and soul.

True, there were some obstacles to their relationship, namely the fact that they lived in different states. But Shelby was convinced they could work it out. They *would* work it out.

She loved him and was almost certain he loved her. Granted, he hadn't actually said the words, but she was relying on her instincts, and every one was telling her that he would.

"Maybe tonight," she said, locking the motelroom door behind her.

She plopped an overnight bag onto the bed and opened it. Very carefully, she lifted out a pale blue nightgown that was more seduction that substance. She smiled.

Tonight would be slow and easy.

Deliciously slow and wonderfully easy.

She lay the nightgown on the bed, then removed a bottle of scented bubble bath from her bag. A long, lovely soak in a hot tub full of bubbles, then she would put on the gown and wait for Travis to walk through the door. Oh, the anticipation was sweet as summer wine and every bit as heady.

An hour later Shelby walked out of the bathroom, shampooed, scented and anxious for Travis's arrival. She slipped on the nightgown and flipped back the bedspread. And waited.

There was a knock at the door.

It couldn't be Travis. He had a key.

"Who is it?" Shelby called.

"Office manager, ma'am. Got a bunch of faxes here for Mr. Hardin."

"Just leave them under the corner of the doormat."

"Okay."

Shelby heard paper rustling, then footsteps walking away. She put on her robe, waited for several minutes, then opened the door and quickly pulled the faxed pages inside.

Normally, Shelby would never have considered reading anything was someone else's business, but her curiosity was peaked when she saw the name at the top of one of the sheets: Judge Neville Alvarez.

Why would Travis get a fax about a Louisiana judge who had been dead for ages? What reason...

Ashamed that she had read even part of the fax, she stacked the pages together and placed them on the desk. As she did, she noticed that the telephone was serving as a paperweight for a piece of paper with a hastily scribbled list.

*Transcripts of trial?*
*Angola records?*
*Copy of death certificate?*
*Talk to Mary Delacroix?*

There was a line drawn through the last question.

Why would Travis want to talk to Aunt Mary? And what trial and transcripts did the note refer to? Judges, prison records, death certificates…what was going on?

Despite a traditional Southern upbringing based solidly on impeccable manners and respect for others, Shelby couldn't ignore an overwhelming tug of curiosity. She began to read the top page of the faxed information. Judge Alvarez was a longtime friend of her family. She remembered him and his wife from her early childhood, so some of the information was a little shocking. Who would have thought kindly old Judge Nev, as all the grandchildren had called him, had been a real carouser in his younger days? This might have made for risqué reading forty years ago, but she couldn't understand why Travis wanted it now.

Her curiosity drove her on though several pages regarding the judge to the next subject—Rafael Perdido.

Where had she heard that name before? Perdido, Perdido… She kept searching her memory as she started reading. It didn't take her long to get a clear picture of Mr. Perdido, a real bad-news character.

The name of the next subject jumped off the page at her and wiped out all interest in Rafael Perdido.

Camille Gravier. *Gravier.* The name Jax had quoted from the bill of sale for the two mares. Travis *Gravier* Hardin. Camille Gravier had to be a relative.

What—a great-grandmother? An aunt? After reading a page or two, Shelby was sick at heart. This Camille woman was nothing more than a tramp. According to the fax, she went for money and power. She was self-centered, greedy and used her looks to get whatever she wanted. Poor Travis. No one enjoyed having their family's dirty linen aired, even if it was over half a century old. Camille's only redeeming grace seemed to be that she was a friend of…Aunt Mary?

*A half a century old. Perdido.* Finally it dawned on Shelby where she'd heard the name before. Perdido, the man mentioned in the files Toni had mentioned. The papers Aunt Mary wanted destroyed, and Shelby had promised not to read. Despite that promise, in light of what she'd just seen, she decided perhaps it was time to take a look at those files and made a mental note to have Toni send them to her.

Suddenly, everything came together.

Rafael Perdido had been convicted of killing Camille Gravier, and he'd been defended by Hamilton Delacroix.

Dear God, Shelby thought, her great-grandfather had defended the man who'd killed Travis's relative!

Shelby's head was spinning with questions. None of this made sense, especially Travis's part in all of it.

No, that wasn't entirely true. One thing was clearly apparent.

Travis hadn't been honest with her.

Whatever his reasons, he had definitely withheld the truth from her. But why?

Why would a man collect all of this information after so many years? What did he plan to do with it? Why rake up details of a murder trial?

She had to know more.

Just then a key turned in the lock, the door swung open and there stood Travis, a smile on his handsome face.

"Hey, darlin', I've thought about nothing but you all—"

The smile drooped when he saw the faxed dossiers spread out on the desk before her. His gaze shot from the folder to the wounded expression in her eyes. "Oh, God," he whispered.

## CHAPTER FOURTEEN

"OH, GOD," HE SAID AGAIN. "Shelby…"

"What is all of this?" She gestured toward the pages.

"I can explain."

"Including why you lied to me?"

She was hurt and angry, and she had a right to be. And it was going to get worse. "Yes."

Shelby stared at him, trying to stay in control of her feelings. Logically, she had known he'd lied to her. The proof was black and white, staring her in the face. But having him admit it was more painful than she'd expected. "W-why?"

He took a step toward her, and she shot out of the chair and backed away. "Tell me why."

Travis knew he was lost when she wouldn't let him come near her. She was going to hate him before it was over, and he had only himself to blame. "I came to Louisiana looking for information about the death of my great-aunt—"

"Camille Gravier. And don't you mean murder?"

"Yes. All my life my grandmother talked about her sister's death as the most traumatic event she'd ever been through. She loved Camille unconditionally. But she always thought…"

He couldn't do it. He couldn't tell Shelby that her

grandfather might be a murderer. It was bad enough that her great-grandfather was implicated.

"Thought what?"

"That Camille, in fact our entire family, was victimized. During the trial, Camille was painted as having loose or no morals. As having driven her killer to murder." That much at least was the truth. "Gran believed her sister was the next best thing to a saint, and she...she blamed the—"

"She blamed us," Shelby said, her logical mind beginning to fit the puzzle together. "She blamed my great-grandfather. And probably Aunt Mary."

"Yeah. Gran spent her whole life hanging on to the hope that someday her family's name would be cleared and her sister's reputation restored. The last hour of her life, she begged me to come to Bayou Beltane and find the truth. I promised her I would."

Now everything was clear. It all made sense to Shelby, except for how trusting she had been. How gullible. "So you came looking for revenge."

It was killing him to see her in so much pain, but they had to get everything—with the exception of telling her about Charles's involvement—out in the open before there could ever be any healing.

"Didn't you?"

"Yes, but—"

"And you used me from the very beginning, didn't you?"

"No. I didn't know who you were until after we...until after you handed me your business card."

"Until after I had kissed you."

He nodded, wanting to take her in his arms so badly they actually ached, but knowing he couldn't. Travis knew her mind would make the next logical progression. He knew what she was going to ask even before she spoke the words.

"Was making love to me part of your plan for revenge?"

"No."

For a heartbeat he saw relief flicker in her eyes, then it was gone, replaced by disbelief. Then anger. "When I think I apologized to you for being so honest, I get sick to my stomach. I can't believe it. What a joke! Why aren't you laughing, Travis? It's funny. Hilarious, in fact."

"Stop it."

"Why? Don't you see the humor in all of this?"

"Shelby, I never meant to hurt you."

"And that's supposed to make everything all right?" She shook her head. "Not in this lifetime. Tell me something, Travis, just for my own curiosity. Didn't your conscience bother you at all to make love to me, when all the time you were plotting against my family? No, probably not. And I, fool that I was, played right into your hands. *I* seduced *you*."

"I tried not to, but you were so sweet and I wanted—"

"Oh, so now it's my fault?"

"No. None of this is your fault." He knew now that she wasn't going to forgive him. "You're right about everything. I am all the things you're calling me in your mind right now. I'm a heel, a bastard, a no-good, lying—"

"You don't get off that easy."

"I didn't expect to."

"What did you expect, Travis? You made love to me. You listened to me tell you how much I loved you and—and…'' Oh, God. She was going to cry. No, she wouldn't give him the satisfaction.

"Shelby, I wanted you then. I still do, but the difference is that I do love you, Shelby. I want to spend the rest of my life loving you.''

"And I'm supposed to believe you? You've lied from the moment you got to town, and now, all of a sudden, you're telling the truth?''

"But I'm trying to explain what the truth is!''

Shelby tossed the fax she'd been reading onto the desk and walked to the overnight bag on the bed. She shrugged off her robe, took out a denim blouse and pulled it on over her nightgown. Stuffing the robe in the bag, she zipped it and turned to him. "You don't know the meaning of the word, but it doesn't make any difference, because I'm leaving.''

"No!'' Travis blocked her exit. "Not until you hear it all.'' She stood in front of him, so still, so rigid that it frightened him. "Your uncle William told me the truth the day before yesterday. He made me understand what kind of person Camille really was. The truth is, she was a tramp. And in a way, she brought her death on herself.''

Shelby blinked. "I don't understand.''

"It's simple. Camille slept with every man who would have her. I don't doubt that she toyed with Rafael Perdido. She probably went to bed with him, then dropped him. And there were probably a dozen other men with a motive to kill her. She used men like Kleenex. She even tried it on your uncle William when he came home for a visit while he was in the seminary.''

Shelby's shocked expression was the first sign that he might have gotten through to her. "She was no good, Shelby. Gran lived her whole life looking at a memory of her sister through rose-colored glasses. I don't know, maybe she knew the truth and refused to believe it. But she went to her grave thinking your family had done ours an injustice. The real truth is a lot more complex, as real life always is.

"Your family paid a high price for Camille Gravier's sins. Your aunt Mary was so sick at heart she left Bayou Beltane for almost a year because of what happened. Hamilton Delacroix did the best he could for Rafael Perdido, and it must have been hell for him when the verdict went against his client."

"It was the only murder case he ever lost," she said. "I always thought it contributed to the heart attack that killed him."

"You just made my point."

The room fell silent, and they stood there, both spent from the emotions of the last few moments.

"Shelby, I've got no right to ask for your forgiveness, but I'm asking, anyway. I love you. I'll always love you. I want a life with you. Marriage, kids, the works."

Her gaze shot to his.

"That's right. I'm asking you to marry me." He glanced down at his boots, then back at her. "Nobody ever accused me of being short on nerve. Brains, maybe, but not guts. If you can forgive me, I'll spend the rest of my life making it up to you."

"Travis—"

"Don't." He held up his hand. "If you answer now, it'll be no. Think about it. Please. I'll wait for your answer as long as it takes, darlin'. Longer."

"I don't know."

"Do you love me?"

"What?" She couldn't believe he was asking such a question after all he'd told her.

"Shelby, you're the most honest person I've ever met. You don't lie. You don't even know how. It's one of the things I love most about you. I'm asking you, do you love me?"

She hated him for asking, but he was right. She wasn't going to lie. "Yes."

Travis didn't even realize he had been holding his breath until she answered. He released it slowly. "Thank God."

"But I wish I didn't."

And with that, heedless of the fact that she wore nothing but a denim shirt over a nightgown, Shelby stepped past him, opened the door and walked out. And Travis very much feared she had just walked out of his life for good.

SHELBY WOKE UP the next morning hoping it had all been a dream, but it wasn't. Every minute of the confrontation in Travis's motel room was clearly, painfully etched in her memory.

She dragged herself out of bed and dressed for work only because she knew that if she didn't she would spend the whole day crying. And while she might feel better at the end of the day, it wouldn't change a thing. No, she *needed* work. She needed to stay busy. Every time she stood still for two minutes, she thought about Travis.

And it hurt too much.

She had thought after her experience with Royce that nothing would ever cause her that much pain. She was wrong.

*Stop wallowing in self-pity,* she told herself briskly, and she dialed Yvette's number.

"Book Nook. Can I help you?"

"Yvette? I'm glad I finally reached you."

"Uh, Shelby. Sorry I haven't called you back, but I've been real busy."

"We need to talk, Yvette. Masson's attorney has presented a revised settlement offer. Even though you may not want it, as your lawyer, I'm legally obligated to make sure you understand the terms. Could I drop by this afternoon?"

"Well, I, uh…today is a really bad time, Shelby. Liz has been handling the store because I've got a migraine."

"In that case, how about tomorrow? We can't stall Trowbridge forever."

"Uh, sure. That'll be fine."

"Say, ten-thirty?"

"Okay."

When she hung up, Shelby stared at the phone for several seconds. Something was wrong. She made a mental note to drop by the bookstore this afternoon on her way home and talk to Yvette. Maybe the pressure of her situation was getting to her. That was understandable. There was a lot at stake for her. Yeah, Shelby thought, maybe a little pep talk was in order.

Twice during the day Shelby almost dialed Yvette again, but changed her mind. They would handle whatever was bothering her this afternoon.

It was almost four-thirty when Shelby finally parked in front of the Book Nook. She figured Yvette would have picked up Dante by now, probably given him a snack, and they could steal a few minutes to talk.

"Hi, Liz."

The young woman spun around. "Uh, Ms. Delacroix. What are you doing here?"

"It's Shelby, and I came by to talk to Yvette. Is she here?"

"Uh, no."

"Will she be back shortly?"

Liz glanced around, as if Shelby's presence made her nervous. "Sure."

"I'll wait."

"Well, on second thought, I think it might be a while before she comes back."

"Which is it, Liz?"

"I—I…" Liz gulped. "Oh, Ms. Delacroix, I'm no good at lying. Every time I try I just make a horrible mess of things. I told Yvette I couldn't do it. I told her—"

"Liz, what are you talking about? What lie?"

"She's not here, and she's not coming back," Liz said, so fast it was difficult to understand her.

"What do you mean, not coming back? I spoke with her this morning and—"

"She was here just long enough to get the last of Dante's clothes, then she left. She's been hiding out for the last few days. Those men came back, and she got so scared, and the next thing I knew she was packing—"

"Packing?"

Liz scurried around behind the counter and produced an envelope addressed to Shelby. "She told me to mail it, but I guess it's all right to hand it to you."

A cold knot of dread formed in the pit of Shelby's stomach as she opened the envelope and read the note inside.

Shelby,
Forgive me, but I'm afraid. Lyle is determined
to have Dante, and the only way I can be sure
he won't get him is to take him away. I know
I'm leaving you in a rotten position, and I really
am sorry about it. But I've got to do this.

Yvette

Gone. Both of them. Shelby had known something
was wrong and ignored her intuition. ''What about
the store?'' she asked, suddenly weary to the bone.

''She said I was the manager now, and set it up
with the bank to pay me a salary. The bookkeeper
does the rest.''

''All right. If she calls you, or comes back for any
reason, please notify me immediately, Liz.''

''Oh, Ms. Delacroix, you're asking me to tell on
her.''

''Let me explain something to you. She will very
likely be charged with kidnapping, and Lord knows
what other charges Masson's attorney will dig up.
They will issue a warrant for her arrest. If she turns
herself in, it will look a lot better than being picked
up by the police.''

Liz's hands flew to her mouth, her eyes wide.

''Exactly. So calling me is the best thing you can
do for her if she calls you or shows up. Okay?''

Liz nodded, and Shelby patted her hand. ''If you
have any problems at all, call me.''

She left the bookstore feeling more depressed than
she had in her whole life, and drove straight home.
Riverwood had never looked so good to her, so wel-
coming. So safe.

Justin hadn't been up when she left the house that

morning, so he had no way of knowing that she hadn't stayed with Travis as she had planned. Shelby dreaded facing her father, telling him, but there would be no escape. There were times, like now, when her perpetually sunny outlook on life was a disadvantage. The last thing she felt like doing was putting on an act for her father. Not that it would do any good. Travis was right. She just wasn't any good at lying. Better to get it over with, she decided, plunking her briefcase down on the table in the foyer.

"Dad?" she called.

"Shelby?"

She looked up and found him peering down at her from the second floor. "Can I talk to you?"

"Sure. Come on up."

A moment later she joined him in the small parlor connected to his bedroom.

"Where's Granddad?"

"He and Uncle William are attending the annual law-enforcement-appreciation dinner that the mayor of Covington throws."

She leaned against the chaise longue, noticing that a photo album lay open. On one page was a picture of her parents.

"Reminiscing?" she asked.

"In a way."

Shelby touched the snapshot of him and Madeline. It had been taken at a party—possibly New Year's Eve, if the hats and confetti sprinkled across their shoulders was any indication. They looked happy. But their marriage had ended with so much bitterness and pain. "Like father, like daughter," she said.

"How's that?"

"I was thinking that you and I haven't done very well in the romance department."

"I don't like the sound of that. Last night you were in love. Today you look…"

"Disappointed," she said. "Hurt and disappointed."

Justin saw the pain in his daughter's eyes, and his heart went out to her. "Can I help?"

Shelby glanced up from looking at the picture. "You can listen."

"Done."

Shelby sat down on the end of the chaise and leaned back against the arm. "He lied to me."

This was covering new ground for Justin, and he decided to follow Shelby's lead. She would tell him what she wanted him to know.

"He came to Bayou Beltane looking for revenge against our family."

"Excuse me?"

"It's a long story, better left for another time, Dad. But the gist of it is that he lied about who he was and why he was here. He thought he knew the truth, but it turned out he was wrong. He admitted his mistake and begged me to forgive him. He even had the audacity to ask me to marry him."

"Did you say 'marry'?"

She nodded. "He said he loves me."

"I'm confused."

"You think you're confused. I'm totally lost."

"Because you're still in love with him, aren't you?"

Tears welled in her eyes. "Y-yes."

"Shelby, I'm not much good at expressing my feelings." He glanced at the photo, then back at his daughter. "I never have been. Can I ask if what Travis did is unforgivable?"

"Of course it is."

"Don't be so quick to answer. Forgiveness is a choice, Shelby. You've had just about everything you ever wanted in life—wealth, breeding, strong family loyalty, friends and a profession you love. You're very fortunate."

"I'm aware of that."

"Up until now." His gaze met hers directly. "With possibly one exception, you've traveled a relatively smooth road. So you hit a bump. This may be a test of your flexibility."

Shelby had never heard her father talk like this. "You think this is about flexibility? Dad, he lied to me."

"I know. And all I can tell you is that the world is not a rose garden or a court of law. It's not always black and white. You have to ask yourself what's important."

"Honesty is important."

"More important than love? If you had to choose between a principle and the kind of love that only comes along once in a lifetime, what would you pick?"

"I—I can't believe you're talking like this."

"Maybe because I've been where you are, Shelby. Just remember that principles are fine and laudable. Certainly necessary. But you can't laugh with a principle, or make love to one. You can't share memories or children."

Justin rose and kissed her on the cheek. "Think about what you want, sweetheart."

Unaccustomed to hearing her father share his feelings so openly, Shelby watched him leave the room, and for the first time she realized that he was lonely. Relating to her father adult to adult was an unsettling experience, particularly when he was able to empathize with her pain. Pain that showed no signs of diminishing.

So what did she do now? Forget about Travis?

Sure. Just pretend he'd never come to town. Never met her in the park. Never kissed her, never…

Pretend he'd never made her feel again.

As soon as the thought formed, so did the tears. Buckets of tears, rivers of them. Her father had asked her if what Travis had done was unforgivable, and Shelby had latched onto his lie and hung on for dear life. Because the truth was too painful to acknowledge.

Yes, Travis had lied to her, but that wasn't what she couldn't forgive. He'd also given her back the joy of loving, then snatched it away. That was his unforgivable sin.

But she wasn't entirely blameless, she realized.

Travis hadn't pursued her. She had gone after him, determined to get back into the romance game. Determined to end her loneliness and find the kind of man who could make her happy. And Travis had. Despite everything that had happened, she had to admit that she had been happier with Travis than she could ever remember being. She wanted that happiness, had gone after it. And when her knight in shining armor proved to be as human as the rest of the world, it was easy to blame him for her unhappiness.

A bump, her father had called it. A test of her flexibility. But out of everything he had said, one statement stood out most clearly in her mind.

*If you had to choose between a principle and the kind of love that only comes along once in a lifetime, what would you pick?*

Her heart didn't hesitate. There was only one choice.

If, as she suspected, Travis had left Bayou Beltane right after she had walked out on him, he might still be on the road. Shelby knew it was late, and that she would probably wake him and his father, but she had to reach Travis. She had to tell him how wrong she had been. How much she loved him. Her fingers trembled as she dialed information for Comfort, Texas. A minute later she dialed the number of the Hardin ranch.

"Is this the Hardin residence?" she asked when a rather sleepy-sounding man answered, presumably Travis's father.

"Yeah."

"Could I speak to Travis, please?"

"He ain't here."

"Then, will you give him a message?"

"If you don't mind waitin' a few days 'fore he calls you back."

"I don't understand."

"He's outta town. Louisiana. Probably be back—"

"Thank you," Shelby all but cried. "Thank you, thank you." And she hung up.

Travis had told her he would wait...

And she knew right where he was.

STRETCHED OUT ON THE BED, one booted foot crossed over the other, Travis stared at the television screen, but couldn't have said what he was watching if his life depended on it. All he thought about was Shelby. All he could remember was the pain in her eyes.

He was a fool to wait, but he couldn't bring himself to leave Louisiana. That decision was too final and far too painful. It meant giving up on what they'd found together. It meant living without her, and he wasn't sure he could do that.

There was a knock at the door. "Coming," he said, expecting to find the pizza-delivery person, even though he wasn't very hungry. Travis dug into his pocket for a twenty-dollar bill as he opened the door. Then he froze.

"Shelby?"

"I, uh…" She shoved the key in front of his face. "I brought your key back."

He took it. "I…c'mon in." He moved back, and she stepped inside.

"Thanks."

He couldn't believe she was here. He didn't care if she had come to tell him what a louse she thought he was. This was his last chance, and he intended to make it count.

"Before you say anything," he said, "I want you to know that I've changed my mind. I'm not going to wait. I'm going to keep after you until you forgive me. Darlin', I'm going to be your shadow. Every time you look up, there I'll be. And every time, I'm going to tell you how much I love you. I do, Shelby. I love you so much. And sooner or later you'll believe me, because—"

"I believe you now."

"No one will ever… What did you say?"

"That I believe you love me. The question is, after all the things I said, do you believe I love you?"

"After all…do I… Oh, Shelby," he said, reaching for her.

She stepped into his embrace as easily, as naturally as she had the very first time, that day she had listened to her heart.

Travis kissed her mouth, her cheek, her throat. "I was scared to death I'd never see you again."

"I love you," she said against his mouth. "I love you so much."

"That's enough to get us through."

"No." She drew back. "I thought it was, but I wasn't being realistic. There are problems."

He pulled her back into his arms. "We'll solve them."

"What about—" He nibbled the corner of her mouth. "Oh, hmm…your father? How's he going to feel about having a Delacroix—"

Travis tightened his embrace. "I know how *I* feel about a certain Delacroix."

"But my law practice is in Louisiana and your ranch is in Texas. How are we—" He kissed her again. And again. "Going to deal with problems long distance?"

"Buy stock in the telephone company."

His mouth was a wicked marauder, making it difficult for her to think. She was trying to be realistic and he was kissing her to death.

"But how will we—"

"You still ask too many questions." Travis kissed her hard, full on the mouth. "There's only one thing that's important, and I'm doing the asking. Do you love me?"

"That goes without saying, but—"

"A yes-or-no answer, counselor. Do you love me?"

"Yes."

"Will you marry me?"

"Yes."

"Those are the only answers I need. The only truth that counts. The rest we'll work out together," he said, and went right on kissing her.

He was right, Shelby thought, melting into his embrace. They could make it work because they had a solution. Love. Strong and enough for a lifetime.

# DELTA JUSTICE

continues with

## *FINDING KENDALL*

### *by Anne Logan*

Ex-cop Remy Delacroix had opted out of
so-called civilisation to live and work in the
Louisiana bayou. But when he finds a
woman left for dead on Willow Island, a
woman who can't even remember her own
name, Remy is forced to become a
reluctant hero.

**Here's a preview!**

# *Finding Kendall*

## *by*

## *Anne Logan*

A BLOOD-CURDLING SCREAM rent the air.

The moment she had awakened, she'd known that something was wrong, terribly wrong. The reality of exactly what was wrong was like the unexpected strike of a venomous snake, and even as the scream died on her lips, paralyzing terror still streaked through her veins.

And the pain... Oh, God, the pain. All feeling, all thought centered on the dull throbbing in her head. Instinctively she realized she should not make any sudden moves.

She tried to open her eyes, but the pain escalated in her head. It would be so much easier to simply sink back into the blessed oblivion of sleep from whence she'd come. Surely this was a dream, she thought as desperation clawed at her insides, escaping in a sound something like a groan or a dry croak. A horrible nightmare. It had to be. Any second now she would awaken, and the pain and confusion would be gone.

All she had to do was open her eyes.

The sound of heavy footsteps suddenly registered. Someone was running. Was this part of the dream?

She *had* to open her eyes.

And when she finally managed it, the pain along

with the sight of a strange man looming in the doorway nearly brought on another scream.

The man was tall, with a raw-boned, sinewy look about him. His sandy hair was sprinkled with gray and had a shaggy, rumpled look about it.

Oh, God. This wasn't a dream. This was real.

"Who—who are you?"

"My name is Remy Delacroix," he said softly.

"Wh-where am I?"

He approached slowly, almost warily. "I found you injured and unconscious on Willow Island yesterday," he answered. "You have a gash on your head and a broken arm. It was almost dark—too late to take you across the bayou to a hospital, so I brought you to my houseboat instead."

"Houseboat? Willow Island? I—I—" Her lower lip quivered uncontrollably and she covered her eyes with her left hand. "What's wrong with me?" She felt tears slide down her cheeks. "I—I can't seem to remember anything!"

"I'm sure it will all come back. Just give it time. Meanwhile, why don't we start with your name?"

"No," she moaned, curling her hand into a tight fist. "You don't understand!" She squeezed her eyes tightly shut. "I can't remember who I am. I can't remember my name!"

# Escape into

Just a few pages
into any Silhouette®
novel and you'll find
yourself escaping
into a world of
desire and intrigue,
sensation and
passion.

# Silhouette

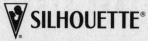

# Escape into...
# INTRIGUE™

*Danger, deception and suspense.*

Romantic suspense with a well-developed mystery.
The couple always get their happy ending, and the
mystery is resolved, thanks to the central couple.

Four new titles are available every month on
subscription from the

# READER SERVICE™